Harbinger

Paul Heingarten

Contents

Revenge Nexus

STRATAGEM AWAKENING

COLLATERAL CRISIS

Published by Decatur Media

New Orleans, Louisiana

www.decaturmedia.com

Cover design by Christian Bentulan

ISBN: 978-0-9972626-7-4

Acknowledgments

To Andrea, my beautiful bride. Thank you for loving me, supporting me, and putting up with me and all my looney ideas, mood swings, and for keeping me from stopping writing all those times I felt like it.

To my family, for their continuing love and support.

To Lisa Herrington, I'm so grateful for you. You, James, and your whole family are simply wonderful. Andrea and I are blessed to call you friend.

To Jenny Bodle, you rock. Thank you for all the chats, the advice, and encouragement as well. I look forward to meeting you in person one day.

To Carissa Andrews, I still miss those Sunday afternoon/evening chats in the Miscreants group! I'm thrilled to be in your circle of writer friends, and look forward to all the things you do in writing/publishing/coaching!

To Sonya and Tony Strong. Thanks for all the advice and suggestions in the indie publishing / marketing world!

To the Bayou Writers Club. I'm grateful for your support as well, and for giving me the encouragement to carry on my publishing journey even when the tides aren't cooperative.

Special thanks to my street team, the "Krewe of Paul" for helping me become the best writer I can. Find out about the Krewe of Paul and get free books at my site www.paulheingarten.com

For Andrea, with all my love

PLACES AND RACES OF LING GALAXY

PLANETS

Agmon

The Far Reach planet of Agmon once shared a similar state to Zormad. Trading markets on this desert planet offer a modest economy for some, but starvation and fear of disease are much more familiar to her residents than survival. Malone Stanton used his limited but growing control of Essence to transform Agmon into a lush paradise, gaining many new followers. Omegana has followed by establishing a post for their Horde on this planet.

Bertold

Sister planet of Delfina, Bertold offers a mostly water covered environment with several islands scattered about. The Omegans have considered this planet in their ever-expanding operations, which involve spreading their military might about for coordinated attacks by what they refer to as their "Horde".

Bimlok Major

While the planet of Bimlok Major itself is largely unremarkable, mostly rocky soil with sparse foliage, the moon of Bimlok Major has been useful to none other than Malone Stanton and his ever-growing collection of devotees. But let's not get too far ahead of ourselves.

Cerulia

Cerulia, home to the Cerulak Race, was another former bustling center of industry in Ling Galaxy in the past. When the Dark Times hit this planet, as it did all of Ling, the rugged determination of Cerulaks to forage and persist gave them a second shot at prosperity, through the repurposing of the spent and discarded items found throughout Ling Galaxy.

Delfina

A mining planet, Delfina also offers a rather arid and bleak environment. Industry on the planet required tremendous indoor facilities for a sustainable quality of life. It is on Delfina that the Railen were relocated by the Universal Alliance (The governing body over Ling Galaxy, also referred to as the "UA") and placed in a former analysis facility as their temporary home, a move that proved to be permanent rather than temporary.

Grondia

This is one of the Central planets of Ling Galaxy and key to the existence of Ling Galaxy and her inhabitants. Lush and tropical in climate, Grondia is home to the Nara and the Spring, where Essence originates from. Essence is the life-giving substance that is harvest by the Nara and delivered to all of Ling Galaxy. Grondia is hidden from most in Ling Galaxy by a dimensional barrier. Only pure Nara citizens are able to travel to and from Grondia.

Omegana

Home to the Omegan race, Omegana is cold and industrial. Metallic structures and cities cover this planet's surface, where the Omegans have developed their abilities and technological capabilities in the cycles since their service to the Nara ended.

Tausian

Arid and desert climate, Tausian is another of the forgotten planets of Ling Galaxy. Former site of a Replication Center, the planet has wandered in recent years into a derelict state. Its native population of Tillians have managed to survive in the lean years, but only barely.

Wenzo

No stranger to the workings of the nefarious, Wenzo's location midway to the center of Ling Galaxy gives it and her residents a key location for illicit trade. Syndicates, organized crime, friendly organizations, thrive and prosper on this dank place.

Zormad

One of the Far Reach planets, Zormad, has a dry, arid climate. Many cycles past, the planet was a bustling center of industry and production. However, changing times mixed with consolidation of industries has left this former metropolis on the far side from prosperity. One of the planet's more prominent native races is the Mardaks.

RACES

Ling Galaxy is vast, with a large collection of races. Here's some of the more common ones.

Celestiak (Lookers)

Celestiak are an offshoot of the Railen race begun by Malone Stanton not long after his escape from prison in Ling Galaxy. In his quest to claim the throne of Ling Galaxy by way of merging himself with

Essence itself, Malone has discovered the ability to travel inter-dimensionally. This gives him the ability to travel across Ling Galaxy in an instant. Through time and careful research, he's been able to pinpoint this ability and has recruited his own team of followers. While he calls himself and his own "children" Celestiaks, the term "Lookers" has been given to them by many others in Ling Galaxy. The Lookers schemes have brought them into the attention of several Lawkeeper groups throughout Ling Galaxy, such as the UA Military and even the Mardak Sentries and Regulation, a force that developed among the Xeno on NewEarth. Finding a Nara is a very important goal to those who want to travel to Grondia, as it is believed the very physical makeup that allows a Nara pure to return to Grondia can be harvested and replicated. Capturing Lookers has been shown to be the only way to effectively eliminate their real threat to the societal and physical order of Ling Galaxy.

Cerulak

A race of scavengers by necessity. Former miners during the period of extensive mining and production in Ling Galaxy, consolidation by the UA left the Cerulaks out in the cold and forced to fend for themselves finding, repurposing, and trading scrap throughout the galaxy. Like the Mardaks, the Cerulaks are fierce survivors, but have been faced with threats from more powerful races than theirs, like the Railen and Omegans. Still, the Cerulaks persist and include in their treks out into Ling Galaxy a search for Railen Trackers. The Cerulaks are more pragmatic about the Railen Trackers, though. They aren't interested in pulling in an actual Looker or a Nara; they just want the quick payoff a Tracker has been known to bring on the black markets of Ling Galaxy.

Mardak

A hardy race, the Mardak claim Zormad as their original home. Their kind are stout in build, with apelike features. Their trades often include those of the trading and scrap business, which they adopted out of a need to replace the economy lost when their home planet, Zormad, fell from its place on the economic boom period of Ling Galaxy. They reside in several cities on Zormad, most notably Tas Ralong, where the seat of their government is.

Nara

Slender, a bit taller than the average human, with a glowing bluish smooth skin, the Nara race has been stewards of the Essence since the beginning of Ling Galaxy. Their life purpose is to develop, process, and deliver Essence to Ling Galaxy. While Essence delivery is essential, it's very common for Essence delivery missions to run into trouble from those trying to capture Essence for their own purposes, while killing any Nara found in Ling Galaxy on their Essence delivery runs. The dangers involved in traveling around Ling Galaxy have required the Nara use various forms of protection, like the Omegans for a time. A force of Nara Security has also handled the chore of protection of the Nara and Essence, as well as a collection of beings known as Scions.

Omegan

Reptilian in appearance and cold hearted in nature, the Omegan race were once servants to the Nara. In their Nara service, the Omegans provided protection for the Nara tasked with sending Essence to all planets of Ling Galaxy. Once the Nara determined the overall danger to their Essence delivery was manageable by their own Nara Security, the Omegans were released. In their freedom from Nara service, the Omegans have grown restless. Through aggressive leaders like Emperor Zakmar, the Omegan Empire is on the move to assert themselves as the dominant race in Ling Galaxy.

Railen

The Railen were originally Nara citizens. Over time, a group of Nara became unsatisfied and even frustrated over how much suffering was taking place in Ling Galaxy, while the Nara only seemed interested in providing the Essence necessary to sustain life. The unrest of these Nara eventually led to an attempted coup and hijacking of the Nara Essence production with the intention of giving Essence out freely to those who needed it in Ling Galaxy, trying to help the famines and general poverty around the galaxy. The Nara guilty of the attempted sabotage were subjected to Disconnection, the Nara process that physically alters law breakers ("Violators") so they are unable to physically travel to Grondia ever again. The Railen were then sent into Ling Galaxy to live out their existence as refugees, unwanted by their birth planet. Their time spent in exile in Ling Galaxy has fostered a spirit of vengeance among the Railen, and their long-term sights are set on reclaiming what was taken from them: access to their home of Grondia and Essence. The Railen are hellbent on finishing what they started many cycles ago and staking claim to all that was once theirs.

Tillian

Diminutive in size, but ever the crafty ones, the Tillian race in Ling Galaxy offers technical abilities in their heritage. Among the scrapping and repurposing races, the Tillians have shown themselves to be very versatile in this work. They don't boast a physical threat, but have been able to make themselves useful, often through trading services on any of the various markets throughout Ling Galaxy, or even in the UA proper - under careful watch by the UA faithful, of course!

Xeno

You know them as humans. Members of an exodus from an Earth on the verge of destruction, the Xeno traveled away from their Milky Way Galaxy and ended up in Ling Galaxy, residing on Zormad. There, they set up a colony called NewEarth and are working at establishing themselves in a new home.

Revenge Nexus

Chapter One

ZOE COULDN'T HAVE CARED ANY LESS what time or day it was. There were too many other thoughts in her mind for useless things like getting up, living a life, and being productive. After all, the living already had it one up on the deceased. Wasn't that enough?

The air in her room was warm, with a touch of dampness. Planet Cerulia had one continuous season of varying heat levels, and this day was no exception to that rule. Zoe swiped her brow and gazed about her abode as she roused herself from her night's sleep, such as it had been.

Zoe's flat was as unremarkable as the rest of the Cerulak accommodations. Zoe had shared this place with Zaratha, two sisters who'd grown up too fast after the death of their parents.

The flickering light of Zoe's wrist comm caught her attention. The message indicated an incoming batch of tech. At least she had work. As part of the Retooling industry in Cerulia, Zoe worked on fixing the spent and partially destroyed tech that Cerulak Harvester crews retrieved from around Ling Galaxy. It was steady work for her and, for the Cerulia civilization, a decent shot at long-term survival.

The old building her quarters took up space in had been fixed, repaired, and cinched far beyond its useful life. The Cerulaks owed their survival to the craftiness and stubborn attitude that, whatever was on hand, could be made functional.

Alongside the wall of Zoe's bedroom stood the beds formerly used by Zoe's parents. They stood upright as if they were wall supports. Cerulia sent items for Retooling once they were ready for discarding. The repurposed items were either sent to Cerulak Zamas military or sold off-world to several interested parties. For Zoe, the discarded beds had more worth for the time being, as they were where both of her parents had taken their final breaths. However, as much as Zoe knew she had to remove her parents' old furniture, she hadn't found it in herself to get rid of it just yet.

A ray of sunlight caught the token on a table towards the doorway to her bedroom. Zoe breathed an uneasy sigh. Just as the beds were for her parents, the emblem was the last memento she had of her sister, Zaratha. Zoe had only heard the news of Zaratha's death two weeks earlier, and the chaos that was her waking life was still unfolding.

Finally, Zoe's hunger motivated her to get out of bed. She paused for a brief stretch. Cerulaks all boasted green complexions of varying shades, with thick hair usually kept in tight braids. Zoe's build was a bit muscular from all her time working in Retooling.

After Zoe worked out the kinks in her body, she started towards the dining console. Still, she paused at her favorite relaxing place: the reclining chair. Zoe used the comfortable seat whenever she needed space and time for thoughts about whatever situation she faced. She kneaded the soft fabric with both hands and leaned over the chair, murmuring unintelligible words, much like a medium trying to exorcise demons. But the words were for herself, and the peace she desperately needed but was always out of reach.

Zoe's wrist comm signaled several beeps, indicating an incoming message. *Probably a status about the Retooling,* Zoe thought. Pon never missed the chance to update her people or, more to the point, be seen on video updating her people. The comm device was a common issue for all Cerulaks. It served various purposes, like identification for all Cerulia citizens and alerts about government announcements and general work schedules.

Zoe activated the Network Console near her favorite chair and watched a report of a space battle on her viewscreen. Swarms of Universal Alliance craft showered the display. It wasn't a shock to see the UA out in force. They certainly had their hands full, with word of the Omegans on the war advance and the Railen stirring up enough trouble on their own. Zoe hadn't pieced together the mechanics of the conflict even before Zaratha's death. She watched the careening Omegan starcraft on screen, engaging UA craft in a deft series of maneuvers and attacks. The sequence of explosions was pretty intense. While Zoe's Cerulak mind had begun a silent inventory of the potential haul from the aftermath, she also found herself more than a little curious about the exact cause of the fight. That was something Network broadcasts never addressed in any meaningful way.

Malone Stanton's alliance with the Omegans had them feeling as invincible as they ever had felt.

The UA had barely contained the Omegan surge so far, other than to shore up Yassel, the central planet of Ling and home to the UA headquarters. *Of course, they're taking care of their own,* Zoe scoffed. *Shame they'd never turn that kind and benevolent eye our way.*

The video from Network switched to an oversized starcraft unloading pallets of building fragments and what looked like engine parts. Of course, not all hauls brought into Cerulia were the same, and certainly not all had weaponry. But, the Cerulaks found ways of getting value in even the most diverse scrap pieces.

In the past, the Cerulaks carried more weight with the UA and Ling Galaxy. As a former key replication center, Cerulia and her Cerulak residents were once a bustling center that hosted the production of items from the basest of essentials to the more complex starcraft for intergalactic use. Zoe only knew about this period from stories, though. Cerulia's period of prosperity, like much of Ling Galaxy, came to a halt once disease and famines throughout the galaxy worsened. The increase in want was more than the Universal Alliance could address, and fighting emerged. The Omegans, Railen, and the various Syndicates were to blame for stirring up most of the trouble from there.

Once Ling Galaxy fell under problems such as famines and diseases like Veculus, the thriving Replication markets slowed and eventually shut down. The UA consolidated Replication facilities elsewhere, claiming a cost-saving measure, further lowering Cerulia and her people into what became known as the Dark Times.

Zoe found a place for herself in the Dark Times of Cerulia. Motivated by her parents, she threw herself into the new Retooling trade. She showed enough aptitude to rise through the ranks and eventually managed one of Cerulia's more prominent centers. However, while Zoe and Zaratha's parents were part of the beginning of the Retooling industry in Cerulia, the business of recovering the lost and spent tech of the galaxy brought a very imminent threat of the bacteria and pathogens sometimes linked with the discarded. The Veculus virus found its way to Zoe's parents, infecting them and making the remainder of their lives a series of bedridden days, in and out of coherence, with only their daughters and a grateful nation watching over them. With her sister Zaratha, Zoe comforted her parents in their final days.

Besides her gratitude that her parents had an end more peaceful than starving to death, Zoe was thankful they weren't there for the loss of Zaratha. One of several victims caught by Malone Stanton while he looked for a Railen Tracker, Zaratha was made a public example, with Pon Ebnora as a witness to the travesty committed on Zaratha and all at the advanced encampment for Cerulia.

Zoe eyed the tray of food, neatly packaged and ready for her breakfast in her food store, and decided against it. With her thoughts of her lost sister also came a pretty disagreeable digestive system. So instead, she opted for a walk to the Cerulak Dispensary for some hot rations; maybe her gastric distress would've eased enough by then.

A choked sob rattled its way up Zoe's throat and out her mouth. She walked on, doing her best to wipe the tears from her eyes and moisture from her nose.

Zoe credited her survival to a few things: love for her sister and an overriding belief in Cerulia. As much as things had soured, she clung to the belief that her parents' work wasn't a waste, nor had Zaratha's. To have said otherwise would've cheapened the lives of her loved ones.

Zoe's continued belief in Cerulia came out most in her work for the Retooling Service. Even the most hardened Cerulak Zamas military couldn't have denied the value of Retooling for Cerulia. Many compared Zamas to a heart; the Retooling Service was the blood. For Zoe, retooling work was simple, the results clear, and the benefits obvious. It was enough that it sustained Zoe through her dark days. Zoe figured her success in Retooling earned her some leeway concerning what she was thinking of asking Pon.

Zoe's town on Cerulia, Rufio, was one of many homes to the scores of scrap Cerulaks retrieved on their various runs. Much of the debris wound up in one of several warehouse structures, formerly replication plants that had long been stripped in the so-called good name of the Universal Alliance, as their efforts were considered more important by the acquiescing Cerulak leadership of the time.

The grey and purple of Zoe's uniform starkly contrasted with the dark and smudged piles of discarded tech and even the service vehicles gliding past the street. Zoe was glad her parents had, at least, gotten to see her promotion to supervisor before they died; showing them her uniform had meant a lot to Zoe.

Zoe's breaths quickened, and she felt her pulse pound in her throat. *It's happening again,* she thought. The feelings started coming the moment she heard about Zaratha. It was a mixture of pain at the thought of her beloved sister dying so brutally and the agony of feeling constrained in her place.

-HELP ME!-

The sound of a voice stopped her in her tracks. It was a male's, but one she'd never heard before. She looked around and saw no one nearby. Zoe shook her head, dismissed it as grief mixed with hunger, and walked on. Her thoughts came at her so randomly those days. It could've been anything.

Zoe smiled a little as she caught a glimpse of Warehouse #13. The towering structure loomed large like all Retooling Warehouses. The number 13 was embossed at the top corners of the structure with bright white paint on a dark gray background.

The air on Rufio, like the rest of Cerulia, was filled with a constant haze. Zoe adjusted the air filter on her mask, a requirement for anyone who worked as extensively with Retooling as she did.

She walked toward the street Warehouse #13 was on and quickly skipped over to the side as another transport hover glided past.

Shouts and giggles broke Zoe's train of thought, and she saw a group of five Cerulak youth who played off to the side of the street. They tossed something between themselves. It looked like a balled-up piece of metal. Their toy was probably a piece of outer armoring for starcraft, Zoe presumed. The faces of the youths clouded with worry for a moment - spent tech was reserved for handling by the Retooling group, but there'd been such an influx lately there was more than enough to catch up on. Zoe welcomed the distraction as a chance to discipline some youth who needed a little straightening out.

"Get that into the receptacle." Zoe folded her arms to compliment her glare. The youth froze for a moment before the one with the metallic piece sheepishly headed to the nearby container.

One of the other youths stepped toward Zoe. "We're between sessions in school. We were just looking for some fun."

"Then I suggest you try the Cove. The tides should be coming in this time of year."

After a few frozen moments, the group regrouped into a game of chase. Zoe eyed them for a moment more before she headed off.

Despite the necessary reminder of discipline and rule-following, Zoe found herself smiling warmly at the thought of how, not that long ago, she and Zaratha would've been right there doing the same thing.

Zoe's thoughts had drifted toward the happier times she had had with Zaratha when the pain hit her. It started as a dull headache but quickly became a piercing agony, so strong she dropped to her knees. She still heard the shouts of the youth off to her side, but they must not have noticed or heard her.

She dropped to her haunches and clasped her head as it began to throb. *What was this?* Had the pains she felt about Zaratha manifested themselves physically? Zoe jammed her eyes shut, and then a dull roar built. She briefly opened her eyes, but nothing changed. Then, a voice came through the din. It was the same voice as before, a male's.

-ZOE, I NEED YOU-

Zoe checked her wrist comm, even though she knew the voice hadn't come from there. Her pulse thumped in her throat. She had no family besides her parents and Zaratha. Her service to Cerulia had been her primary devotion, but this voice scared her.

Who's doing this? After a few moments, she picked herself up, and that's when she felt the soreness in her legs. Apparently, she'd fallen harder than she had realized. With a slightly wobbly walk, she continued. Her grief journey had been anything but pleasant, and now it seemed there were hallucinations to go with the sadness. Could that have been it - her pain of loss manifesting as voices, maybe even Zaratha's, from the beyond?

Zoe trudged on, hopeful that the voice wasn't the breakdown she feared was in her future.

Chapter Two

THE DISPENSARY IN RUFIO TOWN offered Cerulaks the basest of nourishment. With no agricultural industry, their cuisine and consumption were made possible through their scrap business and more or less effective trading attempts. A continuing alliance with the Tillian race made more food available to Cerulaks. Beyond that and the token offerings from the UA, good old Cerulak shrewdness filled the remaining gaps that kept Cerulia above the starvation line.

A steady stream of Cerulaks headed into and out of the Dispensary building. Some were Harvesters sent out with orders for new runs in Ling Galaxy. Others were Retooling workers, going to their morning shifts, or coming in for their meal like Zoe.

Hayaat Munillo, a Harvester team lead, met Zoe as she neared the Dispensary entrance. He was tough to miss, wearing the trademark visor scrap harvesters used for the quick field assessment of tech items.

Hayaat beamed when his eyes met Zoe's. "Hey, there she is."

Zoe offered a polite smile in response. It was her best effort when her most common urge those days was to lie down and scream. "Yep, here I am."

"How are you doing?"

Zoe recognized the tone in Hayaat's voice. It was the same others used for that question to her: drenched with a definite amount of pity and hope the answer that came back wasn't too long. She planted her feet firmly and took as steady a breath as she could. She knew there was one response that satisfied the question without further probes into her lonely, sadness-enveloped hours. "Hanging in there. Got a shift. That tech won't reassemble itself."

"It sure won't. Don't worry; we'll keep you in good supply so you'll never be bored." Hayaat said.

Given the move away from revelations of her usual lachrymose moments, Zoe switched gears on the conversation to more mundane distractions. "What's the food offering today?"

"Tausian cutlets and something they're passing off as soup. It reminds me a little of this waste dump I was in not long ago."

They shared a laugh that was more Hayaat's than Zoe's. Through the brief moment of levity, Zoe noticed the concern in Hayaat's eyes. It wasn't a surprise. Hayaat knew Zaratha more than a little from the runs he had made, with people like Zaratha in support.

"You look more like your sister every day."

Zoe's breath hitched, and she quickly glanced downward and cleared her throat, hoping her emotions weren't too noticeable. "Just so happens I'm still related to her and all."

Hayaat's smile faded a bit. "You know, I could've been with her when she... It's a tough life we've got. Each of these losses stings."

Zoe had received lots of condolences, and while she appreciated the kind words, the most stinging ones involved talk of her sister like she was a stat. It reduced Zaratha's and the other deaths to the order of scrap Ceruleks hauled back. How would Hayaat or the others have felt if one of their deceased family was treated with the simplicity of a piece of molded metallic housing?

Zoe nodded. "Yeah, it stings. I just wish it hurt for Pon."

"I'm sure it does. Things have been moving, with Retooling getting Zamas up to full strength. But, despite that and general welfare improvement, Pon has a way of not spending too much time on any one thing. I don't know how she does it. I sure couldn't be a leader like that."

"My sister and the other Cerulak deaths didn't seem to bother her at all. Besides, I think we haven't been told everything about that raid by Malone."

"What do you mean?" Hayaat's friendly gaze gave way to one of disbelief.

Zoe shrugged. "It just seems pretty convenient. There was a small contingent of Zamas, but not enough for a defensive position. That said, why make a risky move like going for a Railen Tracker?"

Among the usual scrap the Cerulaks hunted, Railen Trackers were a desirable but elusive target. While Zoe and the other Cerulaks hadn't figured out the purpose of the trackers, all appreciated their value. To any race that clawed for survival like the Cerulaks, the payday for a Railen Tracker was tremendous. However, the average Cerulak's interest in the trackers stopped short of their street value. Instead, their sights were on restoring the independence of Cerulia, even from the UA, which had mainly functioned as a figurehead of late, offering sporadic military protection from the ever-growing chaos around Ling Galaxy.

Zoe continued, "Could Pon be holding back information? Maybe we've got more military available to us than she's letting on."

"Pon wouldn't have risked a Harvester crew if she didn't feel like there was ample protection."

"But did my sister's Zamas group have enough available support? She was a ground troop. What about starcraft?"

"Zoe, they had starcraft with them. I'm sure the updates Pon gives would've shared information like that. Why would she lie when every bit of positive news only improves the morale of Cerulia on the whole?"

Zoe watched a group of Retooling workers head out of the

Dispensary. They worked at a different warehouse but wore the same grey and purple uniform, only with a 45 stitched on their shoulders, indicating their home facility. She glanced back at Hayaat, his eyes full of concern.

"Zoe, if you want more answers about it, talk with Pon. As for Zaratha and her group, what I heard is they had just sent back details on where to find some Railen Tracker that Malone was after all along. Other harvester crews have picked up the hunt since using coordinates Zaratha herself sent back. This situation evolves quickly - you must remember, we're not the only people in Ling Galaxy out to grab any spent pieces of tech we can find."

"Hayaat, I really should eat before my shift. I'm allowed to meet with Pon anyway. I'm supposed to collect Zaratha's personal effects, and I've been neglecting that."

Hayaat nodded. "Of course. Hang in there, and please let me know if I can ever do anything."

Zoe gave her best smile and said goodbye to Hayaat as she entered the Dispensary.

* * *

Zoe made her way through the food lines in the Dispensary Complex dining area. The Tausian cutlets Hayaat mentioned looked a little dark for her liking, but her hunger pangs convinced her to try them. She grabbed enough for a meal. She headed towards the common area with a full decanter of Aquand, a common beverage throughout Ling Galaxy that mostly resembled water. The lines of tables in the large hall provided ample seating, and a healthy general roar of the crowd as the assembled ate and made conversation with their table mates.

Zoe found a spot without anyone sitting too close – hopefully enough for her whole time there to be left alone. Instead of making for any chats, Zoe focused on eating. She tried to ignore the image on the video screens along the far wall as best she could. It was Pon

Ebnora with her regular update to Cerulia on the growing conflict around Ling Galaxy and the state of the Cerulak resurgence. Zoe always hated speeches. They didn't happen daily, but they were a part of Cerulak life. Government figures, mostly Pon, talked about plans for the future, and military leaders shared information on threats and how they handled them; these talks came up more often than she liked.

"Got room for another?"

The gruff male voice startled Zoe at first, but she recognized it immediately. As much as she would've liked the solitude, the truth was a few people in Cerulia were always welcome company for her. She smiled for having an even better reason to ignore Pon's video update. "Hi, Quintus."

Genetics gave Quintus Bala a broad and well-developed frame, but his service with the Cerulak military as a heavy weapons specialist hadn't done much harm. He sat the tray next to Zoe's and eased himself onto a spot next to her.

Zoe felt a slight bit of gloom lift around Quintus. He was a regular part of her childhood when she and Zaratha were playmates with Quintus - most likely in the place of those youths Zoe had seen on her way over, playing with pieces of scrap and solving all the problems of Cerulia and Ling Galaxy in the span of a play session.

Zoe took a thoughtful sip of Aquand before she eyed Quintus again. "I don't know what I'd do without you and the Retooling service to keep me focused."

"Always nice to have something to focus on." Quintus' arms flexed almost as if they'd been listening separately from the rest of him.

Zoe arched a brow. "So, got some big maneuvers ahead?"

"Something like that."

Zoe stabbed the cutlet on her plate in thought. "Busy busy. Me too. I got an early notice we'll be handling a huge starcraft this morning. Lots of life support and weapons systems to reconfigure."

"Long as we get the first crack at them. Keep those grubby Syndicate hands away," Quintus nudged Zoe.

Zoe laughed in response. "Yeah, for sure, Cerulia first, right?"

"Yep. Of course, the Tillians are a close second."

"True." The Tillians had suffered during the Dark Times like the rest of Ling. But, unlike most other races, the Tillians had forged a bond with the Cerulaks. Their shared industrial backgrounds made them easy partners, with similar minds for prioritizing in a time when even the simplest supplies were far from easy to obtain. As a result, the two nations' alliance held fast when even the UA's promises often rung hollow.

"Yeah, we wouldn't have had our warehouse setups were it not for Tillian crews helping with refitting our machinery." Zoe sighed before she took a deep swallow of her drink.

She looked back at Quintus, whose eyes had shown more of that glint of concern a little too familiar to Zoe. "So... how're you holding up otherwise?"

Zoe looked away. "I dunno. It still feels weird, her being gone. We fought before she left, you know."

"Oh boy."

The scene had played in Zoe's mind a lot in the last few days. She and Zaratha had taken a few days and gone to the Cove for some relaxation before Zaratha shipped out. It, sadly, wasn't peaceful for long once their conversation drifted towards Zaratha's mission. "Zaratha said we needed to stick ourselves out there more, not let the Omegans get too big or cocky. I told her she was just paranoid."

Quintus' voice lowered a bit. "Was that your last talk?"

"Mmhmm."

Quintus slid his arm around Zoe's shoulder. She winced, not from the touch but from the memory of her last exchange with her sister. Like Zoe, Zaratha also threw herself into her work with Zamas, but their respective efforts at pushing past the grief caused a divide between the sisters. Zoe clung to the belief of carrying on her parents' work, that Cerulia's success depended on rebuilding their economy. Zaratha saw the only path to peace through the end of Malone and an aggressive stance toward him at all costs.

"Sorry dear, that's awful."

"Yep." Zoe dabbed an eye. "I promised myself I wouldn't cry in the dining hall anymore."

Quintus pulled Zoe closer into a half embrace. She leaned her head on his shoulder in response.

"It's OK. I miss her, too. I still remember when we trained together. She always had more of a mind than just for the grunt trooper stuff. It makes sense she'd have gone with a Harvester group as advanced security."

"But, Quintus, they should never have been that far out without more support than they had. As threatening as the Omegans have gotten, I would've figured they'd have had way more starcraft and garrison for defense."

Quintus gazed at his food in thought. "Can't say I'm all in the know, but the units I'm with are mostly supplied up."

"But, our military isn't half as strong as it was at its height, and even that wasn't saying much," Zoe sighed.

Zoe saw a flash of Zamas pride in her friend's eyes at the challenge to the Cerulia military might. "Hey, we're tougher than you think. And, don't forget, they faced Malone himself. He's not exactly an amateur."

"Quintus, we've known each other since we were kids, and you and Zaratha trained together. Unfortunately, Malone is going to keep doing things like this to people. Until someone stops him, we're just going to be in some big pool, hoping we're not the next to get caught in his sights. It's just wrong."

"Zoe, he isn't going to get away with it."

"He has so far," Zoe looked at Quintus through tear-moistened eyes. "He just slips away, nothing doing." Zoe knew Quintus couldn't argue that. She spent lots of her free time watching Network reports; lately, Malone was all over the data stream. He had made a huge splash when he singlehandedly rejuvenated planet Agmon from dormancy into being as lush and vibrant as any place in Ling Galaxy. A cult of followers had emerged for him, too. Zoe never figured out why when Malone had been known as a Nara fugitive and cast out of their race.

"Oh, this is no good. I'm sinking again. Talk to me about something else."

"Like what?"

"I don't care. Anything. Even gear specs."

"Gear specs?"

"Yeah, sure! Never know when I'll have to remember something for a retooling job." Zoe prided herself on her memory of parts and specs over various categories. As the Retooling Service never had the slightest idea of what the next batch of tech they'd receive would be, it was not only helpful but essential they had as thorough an understanding of the variety of tech in Ling Galaxy as possible. While the high-functioning Macro Processor systems had complete knowledge, Zoe had more familiarity with tech than the average Cerulak, including several of her superiors in the Retooling group.

"Thought you'd find this interesting. Remember those two I talked about, Brynn Mak and Zakk Goulden?"

"Oh yeah, real hardnoses. What about them?"

"Well, they were talking at the hanger the other day. Some jabber they heard on Network about the far reach planet of Zormad and the trackers. It seems the Railen and Omegans stirred things up over there. Brynn's got a nose for these things, so they're getting a squadron of ships headed that way. It should be something interesting."

"All I know about those Trackers so far is they cost my sister her life. So, what are they even for, and why are so many people crazy about getting one?" Zoe asked.

Quintus shrugged. "They're part of that hunt for Essence that's going on. Malone, of course, is one of the high-profile types looking for Essence, but others are in that game too."

"So, they're trying to hijack Essence and make the rest of the galaxy depend on them for it?"

"Pretty much. As bad as things are in Ling Galaxy, anyone who controls Essence can demand anything they want."

"Well, why doesn't Pon just go for that? Why are we worried about rebuilding our tech through Retooling?"

"Small steps first. Pon doesn't want to face the Omegans or the Railen until we've more legs to stand on."

Zoe nodded. She always dealt in piles of tech; all of it had some sort of value or another. But Railen Trackers were hoarded so much they were never part of the hauls of any Scrap Retrieval. Only the forward groups in Ling Galaxy had a shot at the trackers.

Zoe managed a weak smile in response. "So, where you off to next?" She hoped Quintus took the hint she dropped in her question, namely, *any chance you can accidentally stow me away so I can help maybe find Malone, which is a little better than being cooped up here?*

Quintus shrugged. "They're sending a unit to the planet Delfina to some abandoned facility. They want to see what they can grab there."

"Oh, the Railen outpost?"

"Former, anyway. Omegans lit it up pretty good."

"Think there'll be any Trackers there?"

"Like we'd get that lucky. No, I'm sure the Railen took those out before their newborn. You never know, though. We could get a few reactor cores if they had to ditch the planet quickly. Those aren't exactly light and portable."

Zoe laughed at the image of even the largest Railen trying to haul a one-ton reactor core on their backs. "Um, no, not really. I've gotten pieces from Omegan assault victims already. They sure don't like to leave a lot that isn't burned to a crisp."

"True," Quintus shrugged. "Not exactly where I'd go on my first hunch. But, gotta realize mining planets like Delfina are notorious for having caverns or underground structures. So, it's at least worth a look."

Zoe nodded and clasped his hand. "Just be careful. I don't want to lose you too."

Quintus placed his hand gently on Zoe's. "I'll watch my six. Just keep the home fires burning here. We'll keep you in good scrap so you won't be bored."

"Good," said Zoe.

Zoe had digested Hayaat's words from earlier a bit, and she felt like throwing the idea out to her friend, at least to get his take on it. The answer was in her mind. What she had to do was clear, but her doubts fuzzed the certainty, so she needed a trusted friend's take.

"I'm gonna ask Pon for a transfer."

Quintus' eyes widened, and his chewing slowed. "Yeah?"

"Yep. I'm already due to collect Zaratha's things. So, it'll be a perfect chance. I'm going after Malone, one way or another. I figure it'll be easier if I get her to transfer me to the military."

Zoe had hoped for a little more support from Quintus, but the look on his face wasn't encouraging. "Zoe, what about your duty to Cerulia and your parents? They worked hard setting up Retooling, and you've already risen pretty high up in the ranks there. Are you ready to throw all that away?"

"I know, it's not easy for me, but I feel like to honor and, more than that, avenge Zaratha, this is what I've got to do. The Zamas must be ready for action like that, right?"

"I dunno, we're really not in the position for forward engagements like that yet. We're getting back on our feet, and, with the retooled items, it's been easier, but that kind of action is still a little out of our reach."

"Well, if I'm out there, who knows? I may just run into him."

Quintus' mouth curved in a half smile. "OK, and what would you do then? You know what he did to an outpost staffed with a squad of trained Zamas."

Zoe shrugged. "I dunno. I just want her to move me to at least one of the scout units. I'm going after him, and I'm not taking no for an answer."

They continued eating in silence for a bit longer. Zoe felt driven, with a specific target in mind, and the more someone suggested an alternative, the more it only irritated her.

"Just remember, we've got to keep our defenses up. I'd love to pulverize the maniac myself for what he did to Zaratha, but we don't have the numbers for a full-scale assault. You know he's in league with the Omegans."

Zoe had even more to chew on, thanks to Hayaat and Quintus. The burning she felt about venturing out remained, though. She just had to figure out a way to get it across to the one person on Cerulia with the power to grant her the right to get the justice her sister and their family deserved.

Chapter Three

A FEW DAYS LATER, ZOE HEADED to the Cerulak Command Center for her meeting with Pon before her evening shift.

Zoe figured her best shot at getting her request granted was to put on an air of respect and deference and do everything short of deep groveling for her assignment change.

The Cerulak Command Center on Rufio town had more than a few scars. The Cerulak history of robust production, interrupted by chaos and many sieges, left not even their central government facility without several lesions. Damage from pulse weapon blasts scored the once proud pillars of the structure, and small piles of rubble stood as jagged memories of the Cerulak fall when their former bustling economy was pillaged and plundered.

The holo image Zoe showed of her sister and the mourning sigil, tradition for any Cerulak who had recently lost a loved one, was enough to gain her entry into the inner sanctum and Pon's area of the facility.

The layout of chairs in Pon's chambers was sparse but still elegant. A series of long tapestries lined the walls in equally spaced locations throughout the room. In the center stood two chairs, one for Pon and an empty one that was evidently for Zoe. She approached Pon and, after the customary greeting, took her seat. The cool air in the room felt different to Zoe. She'd been accustomed to the mild warm air of her abode and the warehouse where she worked.

As much as Zoe craved and even imagined how this meeting and her request would go, her nerves flared when she found herself in the actual moment. Maybe it was the noticeable drop in temperature compared to the other buildings she usually frequented. Whatever the cause, she felt the anxiety work its way through her.

"Thank you for seeing me like this, highness."

Pon offered a warm smile in response. Then, she called in an aide to bring the box of items to Zoe. She would've otherwise dismissed the collection that looked back at her as trash needing simple disposal. But, Zaratha's last effects weren't regular items; at least, not to Zoe.

The assault on the encampment must've been much worse than Zoe had heard. Not many items in the case weren't partially or mostly singed. Black char marks were a common motif in the collection. Still, there were fragments which Zoe's glance drifted towards: a carving of their family crest, Zaratha's uniform insignia, and a twin of the metallic token Zoe made with Zaratha as a sisterly bonding gesture. Zoe gripped the box firmly and gave a deep sigh. What remained of Zaratha was in Zoe's hands, and she knew she'd cherish the items in whatever state they were in for the rest of her days.

As Zoe gazed at the container on her lap, Pon spoke again. "I still remember all the work your parents did, setting up our retooling units and facilities. The Tillians did their share, of course. I know how much Cerulak blood, muscle, and effort were involved. It was a long process, but it's how we'll get our strength back in the galaxy."

Zoe lowered her head. A few moments later, she felt Pon's hands on her shoulders and Pon's warm breath as she spoke softly, close to Zoe's ear. "You've had a rough turn. Don't think I haven't seen that. I wish we could be over this plight like anything, but the simple truth is: without Retooling, we'll never return to a life close to what we once knew."

Zoe's heart clenched at the phrase 'life close to what we once knew' since that was a sad and cruel joke for her. Without her family there, the only way she could return to that life was by dying herself, and even then, she wasn't sure what would happen. There wasn't much for Zoe to cling to except the cause, and even that grip had slipped recently.

Pon returned to her seat. "I hope you know how awful I feel about what happened to your sister. I intend to make Malone Stanton pay for what he did to her and our people."

Zoe felt slightly better hearing about Zaratha through Pon's words, but she knew the retribution she craved required much more than thoughtful rhetoric. She gently moved the box to the floor near her feet and gazed at Pon.

Zoe shifted in her seat as she felt her gut tighten further. As many times as she'd rehearsed this moment, the words were still stuck inside her, so she forced others out. "I've been working hard, the retooling efforts continue, and I'll have another shipment of weaponry ready for our shock troops in several days."

Zoe sent all her possible positive thoughts out in the vain hope that, through some osmosis, Pon heard Zoe's overriding wishes and immediately granted her transfer, even gave her a weapon for her speedy mission to eliminate Malone.

"Highness, with all due respect, I enjoy the Retooling Service, and I appreciate your confidence in me through my promotion, even ahead of some with more seniority. But, I see my sister all the time: when I'm awake, when I'm asleep; the image of her death haunts me. I'm distracted in my work, and I feel I'd be best suited in a forward Zamas unit pursuing the bastard, Malone Stanton."

Pon's eyes flickered, and her lips pressed together before she replied, "Malone is too powerful for us. We must strengthen our position first, and we still need Retooling more than soldiers. With our current troop strength, our best bet is for a solid defense. We must build further to be able to handle forward engagements. I don't want to lose any more like Zaratha and her group. Vengeance is a powerful motivator, but not if it's blind. Zoe, I know how much you want to exact your revenge. I'm negotiating deals with not only the Syndicates but the UA. Their goodwill efforts towards us have been small, but their investment in our supply chain gives us hope that we can finally become the independent nation we once were. The Retooling Service is the only thing that will guarantee our future and, as a valued retooling asset, I can't see fit to grant your request. I'm sorry."

The rejection hit Zoe harder than she thought it might. In all her mental run-throughs of the conversation with Pon, she figured there was at least some possibility of getting a no, but hearing it most definitely was a slam more than she'd expected.

Zoe sighed and thrust herself back into her seat as Pon continued, "I've heard stories like yours from many of our people. Their lives were ruined by what we've suffered during these Dark Times. But, all you have to do is think of the Railen. They languished for twenty cycles on Delfina. Then they followed the words of that maniac, Ander Pimm, and lashed out at the Omegans. Now, they're a race of Nomads, floating free in Ling Galaxy and, most likely, will one day be incinerated in the crossfire between the UA and Omegans."

Part of Zoe, the youth who grew up under the Cerulak banner and believed in the strength of her people, heard what Pon said and knew it was the truth. The Railen had been dealt their own hard blow as exiles from the Nara. And the Railen went the way of seeking vengeance by any means necessary, and it ended up costing them their world. The Cerulak youth had slowly increased in numbers, and while Zamas also grew slowly, it would be more formidable in future cycles.

But, the other part of Zoe, the one who mourned her sister's loss and wanted revenge on a scale not even the Railen were capable of, knew the only way she would ever feel peace again was once she stood over the cold dead body of Malone Stanton, killed by her hand. So, Zoe tried again, her voice more emotionally shaken than previously. "Highness, again, I request to be reassigned to the Zamas units for hunting down Malone and bringing him to justice."

Pon's eyes widened. "Zoe, I appreciate your determination and energy. But, you must remain where you are for now. Don't worry. Malone isn't going anywhere, and I suspect there'll be good chances for you to see him before this is all over."

Pon's word was final, but only on the reach of the Cerulak world. But, Zoe wondered, *what else can I do? I've never been off-world enough even to know where I'd go. Traveling through Ling isn't going to be easy.*

The realization settled on Zoe that her play was a bust for the current round. She picked up the box of Zaratha's items and left for home. She had time before her next shift that evening, but not enough to digest her latest blow of Pon's rejection and where it left Zoe.

* * *

Back in her abode, Zoe wondered if Quintus could've helped her. Quintus had his own back to worry about, though. She wasn't sure if ditching their heritage and Cerulia for a wild goose chase that could end up killing them was an idea Quintus would ever consider.

Against her better judgment, Zoe activated the screen that connected to Network. After a few moments, some updates collected and presented themselves in front of her.

"Show me Malone Stanton," Zoe called out. She smiled as the screen shimmered slightly. Typically, the sift would've prevented reports coming through that hadn't been specifically about Cerulia. But, Zoe had become practiced in altering this, so her searches on Network were less restricted.

The screen became a blur, a jumble of pictures, text fragments, maps, and several national flags. Then, Malone made a speech on planet Agmon, where he restored the desolation to a place with food and even a future.

Zoe browsed the reports beyond Malone, but they became a jumble of scenes that only confirmed for her what she already believed. While other planets seemed to be at the ready call of the UA, she'd never seen any of them set foot on Cerulia. She wondered if the UA even knew they still existed. Clearly, the UA and Ling Galaxy didn't care for her, much less Cerulia.

Zoe settled into her makeshift bed as soft sobs overtook her. She felt adrift, a ship without a course. Her pain had become a companion for her. She wished she knew of a way to get around it, but in an odd sense, it was also comforting. All that lay ahead for her was her work. Pon's rejection stung, but she'd started getting used to these downturns.

Zoe found herself trying to cling to that love of country she'd known all her life, but it felt like it was slipping. *I have to do something, but what?* she thought.

She knew, as much as she wanted to dismiss Pon's sincerity toward her, that Pon had the best in mind. Zoe hated how stuck she felt, but she was. She had to focus on making it through to the next day, the only thing that gave her any direction for the time. Maybe one day it will be different.

Zoe grabbed the token from its resting place on a shelf near her bed and pulled its more tarnished twin from Zaratha's box. Zoe clasped the curved metal pieces in one hand. They caught the light in the room, and the etchings on both still showed up after all the time had passed. The Cerulak words for sister and eternal bond brought more tears to Zoe's eyes. *I can remember her even if she's not here,* Zoe thought.

I'm all that's left of the Enix family. I'll see a way through this. If I have to work my way up to being a Cerulak leader one day, so be it. But we'll rise out of this place. Things will be better; there will be more to this life than what is here already.

A dull boom jarred Zoe out of her thoughts. Her mind switched gears from wallowing to the moment. Retooling was a messy business; sometimes, a ruptured reactor core made it back to their warehouses. But, something in Zoe's gut had her thinking otherwise. *It could be a weapons test*, she thought. The Cerulak military did them from time to time. Sometimes, even the best retooling job needed a little bit of verification.

Her mind still dissatisfied, Zoe tapped the comm device on her wrist. The small bracelet displayed a feed of the security video systems at her warehouse. There'd been a report of some activity, but the scans done by personnel on site only returned reports of possible energy discharge from some fuel cells. It wasn't unheard of, as retrieved starcraft parts often included fuel cells. Zoe was about to settle back down when another pain, like the one from earlier, hit her. However, this one was much more intense. The voice she had heard before was back, but it was far more detailed this time.

-ZOE, COME TO WAREHOUSE 13 NOW-

Zoe felt her neck go cold, and she froze with fear. She had it with theories; it was time for solid facts. Her shift wasn't due to start for another two hours, but that was too long to wait for answers. So, she grabbed her suit, a handful of rations, and a pulse pistol for good measure before she set out into the late afternoon air of Rufio.

Chapter Four

THE STREETS AROUND ZOE'S NEIGHBORHOOD were empty. The skies were clear, and the blaze of their orange sun was enough to warm the air around her. The burnt stench of transport exhaust fumes hung in the air. The only sound that would've filled the air during the day was the occasional transport and a few of the youth on their Skipper vehicles, light and nimble hovers that traversed the grounds away from the streets and pathways.

Zoe arrived at Warehouse 13, checked in, and headed for the shift supervisor's console. Sasika Pettet sat at the desk connected to the bank of computers. She had shown promise from back when she was a rising cadet in training, but Zoe had noticed, since her assignment to Warehouse 13, that Sasika also suffered from strict attention to procedure. In most cases, that would've been a big plus, but it only annoyed Zoe at the moment.

A series of holographic images danced in the air as Sasika worked controls on the board. Zoe made it to the desk without the slightest reaction from Sasika. However, Zoe startled her out of her work-related trance when she spoke.

"Situational awareness is a good thing, Sergeant Pettet."

"Aye, Lieutenant Enix." Sasika's breaths were still hurried as her initial shock wore off.

Zoe looked at the console, where a video scan of the facility was underway. "We've got security measures in place, but there's no way of knowing when someone might circumvent them."

Saskia removed her control visor. "Of course, Lieutenant."

Zoe glanced over from Saskia's worried eyes back to the console. "What's the building status? I got an alert and headed right over."

Saskia wiped her mouth and shrugged. "Looks like an unstable core in the starcraft wing. I've ordered it sealed as a precaution until we get the source mitigated."

Zoe knew the next move would be for a drone review of the area to identify the exact source and determine the best course for containment. But, Zoe had other ideas in mind.

"I'll check it out. Stand down on the drone probe. Keep your comm open, and I'll call back with a status."

"But, Lt. Enix. The standard procedure?"

"The procedure, Saskia, is to have these ships ready in time. Need I remind you we're expecting our Zamas Military here in a few days to collect another batch of repurposed starcraft? I won't leave anything that important in the hands of a drone. There are too many variables at play here. It takes less time for me to sort it out. So again, stand down and keep your comms open. I'll contact you again if there's any trouble."

"Aye, Lieutenant Enix."

Zoe strode off from the console and down the wide corridor. The admin section was at the warehouse's outer layer, consisting of several shells of protective walls. Retooling work brought several hazards, which required extra levels of protection. The Tillian architecture provided the Cerulak facilities a measure of safety, but their protocols fulfilled the rest of the equation.

Zoe first passed a collection of armored pieces lined up neatly on a series of racks. They were once parts of starcraft outer casings, fabricated building parts, and spent reactor cores. Any tech in the outer area was deactivated from any powered charge and considered harmless, ready for perusal. The inner section of the warehouse was reserved for tech still somewhat functional and, therefore, at higher risk for accidental energy discharge.

Once Zoe arrived at the portal to the inner section, she looked behind her to the shift console and Saskia - both had become pretty small in the distance. The console was the management point of the warehouse and the main point where Zoe and her team handled all receipts of tech and their subsequent release. It was the common resting place during a shift and where Zoe would be soon enough. But not before she solved the mystery her mind wouldn't let her forget.

After several more minutes, she arrived in the starcraft wing. The graceful vessels stood in a row, their respective fuselages decorated with varying levels of charred burns. The first few crafts Zoe passed were on the rehabilitated side. While many still showed superficial scoring marks, these starcraft were internally repaired and vetted. Cerulia wasn't out for cosmetic beauty in her starcraft, as long as structural integrity was guaranteed. The ships were also fitted with the crest of Cerulia and would see service very soon, with Zamas troops heading in for the latest shipment. But Zoe's gut told her this wasn't where she was supposed to look, so she continued on her walk.

Past the refurbished craft, through another series of reinforced doors, lay a batch of the newly received. Each of these ships had various amounts of damage, from minor breaks in their outer shells to near-total mechanical dismemberment. These starcraft's outer casings were unique collections of mechanical carnage, each with a series of fractures, blast charring, and breaks and tears through the outer hulls that rendered the craft in some way or another useless. That is, useless until their harvesting by the Cerulak crews for Retooling. The air in the inner room was danker. Shift workers would be around at some point, lighting the area and filling the musky air with the sounds and smells of Retooling work.

The noise of ruffled fabric jolted Zoe to a quick stop. She extended her light, but she only saw the dull armoring of starcraft around her.

"Who's there?" Zoe hoped her voice had more authority behind it than she felt. It could've been an errant worker, caught up in their day before they realized the time. *They should've known better than to play games like this.*

Zoe continued slowly through the pathways between the ships. If this was someone from the Retooling team, they were on their way to disciplinary action.

A small collection of tubing cascaded to the floor behind Zoe in a loud crash. Fear tightened her chest as she spun around, her hand firmly around the handle of her weapon. She neared the sprawled tubing and took a few short breaths. "Last chance, I'll fire on you if I have to. Show yourself now."

Zoe unholstered her pulse pistol and stepped around the nose section of a cruiser when a pair of piercing blue, glowing eyes stopped her short. She flung her light around, but the beam only lit up the darkened hood and cape of the figure as they stood only a few feet away.

"Who are you; what do you want?" Zoe shouted. A million thoughts raced through her mind. A far-fetched part of her mind would've admitted that she considered for a moment that it was somehow Malone. *I'd heard he's got telepathy. Maybe he tracked me here after he killed Zaratha.*

But the figure said nothing. Instead, it just plodded forward. Zoe took a measured step back. "Don't come any closer. I'll shoot." She aimed her weapon at the center mass of the dark figure and waited.

The figure stopped. Finally, in an echoed voice, it said, "I'm not here to harm you."

"I'll decide that for myself. Let's start with what the hell you're doing here?"

The figure shifted its hood and gave a series of heaving coughs before it replied. "I was hoping you'd tell me."

The deflection annoyed Zoe. "Were you a prisoner on board a craft? All the ships in here were taken from -"

"- space and their field of use, yes. I'm aware of the Cerulak way. I suppose that's the answer we're both looking for."

Zoe nodded. "Typically, a craft is cleared of all life forms before it's returned."

The figure responded with a chuckle that quickly devolved into more coughs. "Well, that's just it. I'm not a typical life form. And, I suppose, my appearance is a bit troublesome."

"More than a bit." Zoe took another step forward.

"I should tell you, whatever stroke it was that landed me here, I know there's a reason for it. And I'm betting it's you, Zoe."

Zoe felt a deep pain in her gut at the sound of her name spoken by a stranger.

"So that was you I heard asking me to help you?"

A slight bow of the head was all she got in reply.

"I dunno how you did that, but it really hurt. Don't do that again, alright?"

"Of course – I'm sorry about the pain, I was a bit desperate to reach you, and I felt it best to contact you using my telepathy. I forget it can sometimes cause discomfort."

Zoe cocked her head. The answers she'd gotten hadn't done much for her ease of mind yet. "How do you know my name, anyway? I don't know who you are. Why do you even care about me? Do you think I'm stupid or something? I'm responsible for thousands of pieces here. I've every reason to stun you and bring you in for disposal, just as soon as I'd bother listening to a word you say."

The figure regarded her with sad eyes. Zoe couldn't read its face under the dark hood, but the slumping of its shoulders made her wonder just what its intention was. Then, suddenly, the figure heaved, and a series of wet coughs echoed around them. "I'm aware of your loss. The Cerulaks, anyway. Your people were ambushed by Malone Stanton not long ago, yes?"

"Yeah, just like anyone who bothered to check on Network would've known. So, what's it to you?"

"It so happens that I'm looking for Malone. I'm actually very interested in him."

"Did he send you here to finish us off or something?"

The figure shook his head. "No, child. Nothing like that. It's true, however, that he... Malone and I were friends in the far past. You see, I was once a Nara, like Malone. We knew each other and grew up together. But, we were both cast out by the Nara forever."

The more the figure talked, the more Zoe forgot about it being a problem for her.

"Please, I'm not well." The figure showed one hand, where a trail of bright green blood oozed out until a few drops hit the floor.

Zoe marveled as the realization set in that the figure was a Nara. "I've never seen a Nara up close before."

"Former Nara." The figure swiped at the greenish liquid that lingered on its lips. "But, if you'd like a more proper name for me, you may call me Pietro."

"Fair enough - Pietro."

"Don't worry. In my present state, I couldn't hurt you even if I wanted to."

Zoe found Pietro's choice of words just a shade less than a mild threat. At least for the moment, Pietro hadn't appeared to be summoning any electrical fields or unsheathing any weapons. Her continued curiosity took care of the rest of her doubt for the time being.

"Let's get back to you telling me why you're in this warehouse, so maybe I'll feel a little better about you being here."

"The best I can recall, I was traveling through space in what I thought was an unassuming craft."

"What craft and where from?" Zoe asked.

Pietro paused for a heaving bout. "I was left in Ling Galaxy to fend for myself. Surely you wouldn't begrudge a beggar scraping by, by whatever means they could get to sustain themselves. My time after exile from Grondia has been a chaotic series of moves. I'm guessing the craft found was near the Far Reach planets. Good enough?"

Zoe nodded, and Pietro continued. "I've got no allegiance to the Omegans, and certainly not to the UA, but I'd hardly be seen as a threat. Or, at least, so I thought. But evidently, my craft was suspicious enough for the UA to haul me in. And, not being one for incarcerations of any length, I decided to try my luck. The result was a heavy barrage of fire directed my way. Through some miracle, my ship was spared, but from the attack and my general state, I was a little too weak and, I suppose, I collapsed - for how long, I don't know. Next thing I knew, my craft and I were brought here; I assume the haul from one of your crews."

Zoe imagined being stranded in space with no one at all. Furthermore, being wounded to the point of being helpless. She admitted that, at least, despite her terrible series of losses, she had a home front that offered her support. People like Quintus and Hayaat and even Pon. Pietro was indeed a lone survivor. She pitied him for it.

"Ok, so you're a Nara. Go on. Why did you leave Grondia? I thought it was a paradise."

"Not leave by choice, child. Disconnection. It's a most involuntary and cruel process. That's mostly to blame for the way I look. The Nara aren't just content to punish those who violate their laws. In Disconnection, a Nara's body is physically altered to prevent return to the home world of Grondia. The planet exists on the other side of a dimensional barrier, through which only Nara and their specially designed craft can cross."

"And yes, other than their draconian penalties, Grondia is otherwise a paradise. Center of Ling Galaxy, where the life of all in Ling Galaxy emanates. I had many responsibilities there once. I was part of the team who oversaw processing Essence until it was made into the Orbs that are delivered to Ling Galaxy to sustain the galaxy itself."

As intense as it must've been for him, Pietro's story still wasn't adding up for Zoe. "Why were you removed from Grondia? Did you kill someone or something?"

"No, in fact, for a good while, I was quite the model citizen. I had the eyes and ears of the Nara machine. I rose through the ranks, blazed through my training, and was ready to ascend to even higher responsibilities. I learned all about Essence and knew as much as my instructors or even more before long. As a result, I was placed in my profession for several years before most of my peers even graduated."

"Malone, on the other hand, was branded a troublemaker early," explained Pietro. "He always had a problem with following even the most basic Nara instruction. His parents were part of a romantic movement among Nara who believed Essence wasn't for us to give away, but for Nara to use for their betterment and ascendence into a new order of consciousness. While I was never about their philosophy, I did see the potential for Essence beyond what the ordained Nara mission was. So, Malone and I eventually came together. His insatiable desire for action, paired with my ability to analyze the facts presented to us. We eventually devoured all the profuse lines of Nara writings about Essence, and all it had to offer via their texts. In those writings, I finally found a truth our teachers had denied us. Malone used my years of ongoing research and formed it into the basest of hypotheses."

"Anyway, I showed Malone my project with Essence. Left alone, it's the source of life in the galaxy. But why would anyone ever leave something that great alone? Surely there are more applications. If this substance can sustain life, surely it has potential for creating it as well. The Nara had in their grasp the potential for ultimate power. Who knew the galaxies that lay beyond Ling? With Essence fueling our weaponry, we'd be a force in the Universe. So why settle for the confines of a single galaxy?"

Pietro's words stunned Zoe. For all her life, her world consisted of Rufio town, her family, and her work. She knew just enough about Ling Galaxy that was filtered to her through the Cerulak sift from Network. However, her worldview had enlarged by epic proportions in just a brief conversation with Pietro. His story filled her mind with other ideas. Revenge was still utmost to her, but perhaps there was more. No one she'd talked with had even mentioned anything like what she'd heard from Pietro.

Zoe asked, "How did Malone turn on you? What happened?"

"Well, once I showed Malone my work, it hadn't taken him long to push me out one day. Finally, he said he had something to show me. So, we met near the Essence plant on Grondia. The huge structure enclosed all the important work with Essence. I remember so much about that day."

Zoe noticed Pietro's voice wavering with the memory. She thought, at first, it was another coughing spasm, but this seemed to be more on the emotional level.

"I asked Malone, 'What exactly are we doing here?' He smiled at me and said, 'I want to thank you, friend, for what you've shown me. It's time we focus our work on realizing the true potential of Essence.'"

Pietro swept aside the folds of his robe and displayed the series of scars covering his body. Zoe gasped in shock at the lacerations and scarred skin that abraded most of Pietro's frame.

"How did he do all of this?"

Pietro winced. "Essence, child. He used what I showed him against me. Before I was ready, he sent a surge through me, enough to disfigure me like this and incapacitate me for long enough for Malone to call our Nara Security force and report me. It's a wonder I wasn't killed by what Malone did. I have to think that was his goal - to leave me alive. Maybe he thought by only maiming me, he'd let me see all he would do from the ideas I fed him. Because I thought he was my friend. It later made sense why we'd been so close to the Essence plant. Malone reported me for Essence manipulation, a most serious crime in Nara law. I was Disconnected and left in Ling Galaxy."

Zoe winced at the wounds and watched the sadness in Pietro's eyes as he adjusted his robe back into place. Malone's trail of deception and murder wound way further through Ling Galaxy and time than she could've ever guessed. Zoe couldn't have imagined that level of brutality. She was hell-bent on getting Malone, but she couldn't have sold out anyone like her friend, Quintus, or even Hayaat for that goal.

"I was cast out of Nara like the Railen and several others. Those who'd committed crimes against the Nara. I was a bastard, thrust into this galaxy and forced to scrape by on my own. Since my exile, I'd heard reports of Malone. He'd been sent to prison because he not only violated Nara rule but was in active plots to overthrow the Nara system. It figures he'd have found his way out of incarceration somehow. Probably convinced his guards to join his cause."

Besides the unbelievable depravity of Malone's ambition, Zoe's mind was stunned by the depth of Pietro's injuries. "How did you survive with those wounds?"

"Oddly enough, the Nara had the smallest amount of sympathy for me. My wounds were treated to the point of sparing my life. But my body was modified, and I was forbidden to return to Grondia from that point on. Since then, I've survived on a moderate level, doing my best to channel Essence in Ling Galaxy however I can. So much of what Malone has in his abilities now, I've been able to do for myself. He is several steps up on me with his Essence orb. And, I'm just not the politician he is, so I don't have the legion of followers he does. But, maybe now my cause will gain momentum, with individuals like you behind me."

Zoe smiled a bit. "I'm a Cerulak. I've sworn an oath to Pon Ebnora and our kind. It doesn't mean I can't support the enemy of my enemy, I guess."

Pietro smiled. "I suppose I can live with that. But, anyhow, there you have it. I've come to regret what I've done, and I know, whatever happens, I must stop Malone. Not for the Nara's sake. They don't care about me any more than they do for their other cast-outs. No, I want to stop Malone because he betrayed me. He stole what I'd developed. He took my plans and used them for his own. And I want your help."

"Show me your face," Zoe said. Her skin bristled at the thought of finally seeing him. Pietro eyed her for a long moment. "How will that help you believe me more than you already do?"

"It'll show you trust me. If you want my help, I must know that you have faith in me. I can't follow someone who won't even show me their face, and the fact you hide yours won't work with me. It's a starting point and something I'm going to insist on."

Pietro chuckled a bit in response. "If I must."

Pietro's hands grasped the edges of his hood, and in one swift motion, he uncovered his head. Zoe gasped out of reflex. Pietro's skin was dark brown, with a series of ridges that looked like scars from a succession of burns. The glow of his eyes hadn't dimmed, even without his hood on. A low amount of stringy grayish hair topped Pietro's head in a random pattern. He managed an awkward smile at Zoe's reaction.

"I don't think I'll ever forget your face," Zoe muttered.

Pietro replied with a combination of heaving and chortling. "I don't suspect you will."

Zoe let Pietro's appearance settle on her for a few seconds longer before her mind snapped back to the task at hand. They quickly needed a hiding place in the warehouse for Pietro if she was to be his accomplice. "Look, there are crews that come by for gear or to drop off another haul all the time. I have to keep this place working. You can stay if you want. I'll find you a spot, but you've got to be quiet and keep a low profile."

"We've got to hide you in the meanwhile. I'll tell the team there's been a reactor leak, and I'm personally investigating it. I'm a group leader here, and the output of this place is on me, so they'll give me a little time to check out something as serious as a reactor problem."

"That shouldn't be a problem. But, I would have an easier time if you had any medical assistance available."

Zoe thought about the supplies at the front office. They kept the most basic of items. Food wasn't exactly a luxury. "I can grab you some med supplies. If you're hungry, that'll take a little doing. We're under tight rations here, but I'll see if I can slip you something."

"Why are you doing this, helping me? Why aren't you reporting me to your superiors?"

Zoe felt her emotions pushing in multiple directions. She knew people like Quintus would've expected her to cut Pietro off, stun him and bring him back. But her vengeful side was an edge stronger. "Because, one day, you're going to help me. I want to kill Malone. I have to find a way off-world, but I've never flown a ship into space."

"How do you think I got around in Ling?" Pietro coughed. "Wasn't easy, but I've seen my way around a few consoles, enough to make me a pilot who won't crash a starcraft anyway."

"Fair enough. So, let's get you well enough for travel again, and then we talk about what you're willing to do to help me get Malone Stanton."

For the first time since she could remember, Zoe saw an opportunity. It wasn't clear-cut and required more than a bit of trust in Pietro. The Cerulaks made it clear they wouldn't be spending time or resources on Malone. While Zoe couldn't have denied this was a dangerous thing in and of itself, she knew there was no way she'd ever rest until it happened.

Chapter Five

ZOE'S WORLD HAD BEEN JOLTED AGAIN with the presence of Pietro. Of the many feelings she had over his company, she felt a solid but odd kinship with him: alone, with no family, and in pain. While his maladies included more physical issues than Zoe's, she admitted it felt like she'd looked in a mirror.

They agreed it would be best for Pietro to hide around the wing with the finished starcraft. Fewer crews lingered in that section than in the area with the craft waiting for rework and Retooling, which would, at least, give them more time to figure out a plan while Pietro was nursed back to health through Zoe's regular delivery of spare rations.

Zoe found enough extra provisions at the Cerulak center to get a small but steady stream of supplies to Pietro. Sometimes it was just an extra bread roll. On other occasions, she managed to grab an extra ration or even some med packs without attracting too much notice. The Cerulaks were in such a hurry to get the latest batch of Retooling done; it gave Zoe the excuse of an occasional late-night shift and an alibi on the extra supplies. The inconsistent documentation of their food was her saving grace.

A few contacts came in via Zoe's comm channel from Quintus. He checked on her periodically, but she resisted replying. She wasn't sure how to explain to Quintus what had been happening with Pietro anyway. Zoe didn't know if she was more afraid of Quintus knowing or telling her something she couldn't have dealt with, like her continued harboring of a mysterious entity would've likely been considered treason.

Nightly, Zoe and Pietro began a ritual. She arrived and headed towards the cargo bay at the far end of the warehouse. The bay had been cleared of radiation by Zoe not long before. Even though she'd warned Pietro of the physical danger, he seemed unconcerned. Zoe assumed he'd been through enough so-called treatment from the Nara and whoever else, that a little radiation was the least of Pietro's concerns.

Pietro accepted the food happily. Most nights, it was a simple nod, and Zoe was off, trying not to linger too long for fear that particular area may have been monitored. The cargo bay walls, reinforced to prevent radiation leaks, gave them an extra advantage as it was easier to trick a scan should any curious Cerulak decide to check for life forms. Zoe wondered if and how Pietro's body would've shown up on a scan. Given what he'd been through, she wondered if he'd still be classified as among the living anyway.

On one visit, Zoe felt it was time for a more in-depth report from Pietro. "How're your wounds?"

Pietro glanced at his arms as he slowly chewed. "I guess they're improving. I sure miss when I was a Nara. We healed pretty quickly from injuries, sometimes within hours. It was the common belief that our proximity to Essence accelerated our healing, even slowed the aging process."

"What was it like, being around Essence like that?" Zoe asked.

Pietro's face lit up with a glow of fond remembrance. "Essence is the true source. The UA Mystics talk about life, but as a Nara, I was very close to the origin of that life itself. It's one thing to have blind faith, but I had visceral proof. I truly long for that again, somehow. But, for now, I'll accept the justice of ending Malone."

"What do we do then? How do we get him?" Zoe felt her face flush with excitement. All the hours spent imagining her revenge, the idea of it happening very soon was almost too much for her to bear.

"Child, if it was that easy, do you think I would've ended up half maimed and on your planet? There're any number of bounty hunters in Ling. The Syndicate alone would've stopped Malone if he wasn't so good for their business. But, you must understand, it takes a lot of finesse to get a target like Malone. This will be a time-consuming effort."

For the first time in a while, Zoe felt a smile come over her face. Her days had changed a bit and hadn't been as filled with sadness, regret, and sorrow. Instead, a tinge of hope blended into the mix, a quite overdue ingredient. Pietro hadn't completely earned her trust, but he had offered her the one thing none of her kind had yet: the chance for revenge.

Chapter Six

ZOE WASN'T SURE IF SHE FULLY BELIEVED Pietro or was just too twisted up about Zaratha's death, but he'd successfully convinced her about the ship caper as a good idea. After all, Pon hadn't offered anything more than some so-called condolences by way of speeches, and assurances that the revenge on Malone would happen, in time. *She's as bad as the UA,* Zoe thought. *Feeding us with enough hope to keep us from starving, but it's never anything other than empty promises.*

While deep down Zoe knew Pietro wasn't a sure thing, he was more driven for action than anyone in Cerulia, except for Zoe herself. She figured he was keen enough to realize Zoe's access to the armory was an asset. Zoe just had to make sure Pietro was on the level about giving Zoe what she wanted in the end. Pietro tried his best to keep in the shadows, which was easy for him.

It hadn't taken Zoe long to rule out Pietro's former ship. Besides being in a condition that landed it in the Cerulak Retooling service, the craft needed a good round of work by the Cerulak crews, which meant a far longer time hiding and covering for Pietro than Zoe was interested in.

Instead, Zoe took Pietro for a look at the retooled starcraft. Each was ready for another excursion into the stars, their hulls gleaming with a redemptive shine.

"Any of these look good to you?" Zoe asked.

Pietro strode back and forth in silence down the rows between the ships. His hands pressed together at his chin. "They're all junk compared to Nara starcraft, but our situation doesn't allow for pickiness."

"If we're gonna do this, it's gonna be on one of these ships, so you better choose."

Pietro nodded and glanced back to the room's far end, where his gaze froze. He signaled Zoe to follow, and he approached the craft. It was dark in color, with some strange markings on its tail. The dim light reflected on the name embossed on the side of the fuselage: *Outspan*.

Pietro folded his arms, a triumphant gleam in his eyes. "Zion class cruiser, pre-Transient Warp era. Even without the latest engine, these ships had enough strength to get around the galaxy quickly. Basic light speed on these would be very advisable. This *Outspan* craft should serve our needs nicely."

Zoe shrugged. To her, all the craft and tech she saw in her place were tough to distinguish between. They were all, in her mind, pieces that would one day be useful again. She felt a little similar to them in that respect. Her life was in a queue, waiting for something to rearrange the broken pieces back together until something fit, something took, and she felt like herself again - or, at least, a close facsimile.

Zoe ran her hands over one of the former blast points on the *Outspan's* structure. "I've heard it said that the repurposed starcraft in Ling are much better - they've proven their durability by taking fire head-on."

Zoe's nerves ramped up a gear. While it felt like she had a great opportunity to get Malone with Pietro, she worried about how stealing the *Outspan* would go down. What if Pietro wasn't able to handle the security? Surely Zamas would've swarmed the place as they left in any starcraft without authorization. Pietro had gotten stronger recently, but she still hadn't seen much in the way of him being a physical threat. If he had any control or abilities through Essence, she hoped he would show them fast.

Zoe's gaze lingered on the *Outspan* when Pietro's voice jumped her out of her semi-trance.

"Are you alright?" Pietro's eyes showed concern. "I'm sensing you're having doubts about this."

"You're saying we can tear across Ling Galaxy, and just the two of us will bring down someone whose rallied thousands of people to support him on nothing more than a promise. I just don't know how much we'll be able to make a difference."

"Even one individual, with enough determination, can make a mark. You have to decide for yourself. Change requires action."

Zoe heard Pietro's words and glanced back at the *Outspan*. In the thriving era of Ling Galaxy, Zion Class cruisers like *Outspan* often made supply runs to all ends of the galaxy. Their versatility made them handy tools for the nefarious, and Zoe mused their little enterprise fit neatly into that column.

"Where exactly are we heading, anyway? Having a course would sure help."

Pietro frowned a bit, his arms folded. He strolled around under their craft. "Malone's been hopping around Ling Galaxy pretty quickly. I say we start with some of the Far Reach planets and work our way in. The fighting between the Omegans and the UA should divert their attention from the Far Reach."

It sounded good enough to Zoe. But, she wished she could've talked with Quintus before they left. Maybe he would've told her it wasn't such a bad idea, doing what she was going to. Or, he would've said she was as nuts as she thought, trusting a strange outcast she'd met days earlier. But, her grief and hunger for revenge obscured the other voices that she'd listened to until the path ahead seemed clear, even if it may not have been.

"Well, let's go with the *Outspan* then," Zoe said. "We can, at least, make a go of it that way."

Pietro nodded. "Load up, let's get star-"

The whine of the large entrance door broke up their conversation. Pietro hissed. Zoe felt her throat tighten as a group of Zamas soldiers walked in. Her frayed nerves worsened when she saw Tarmun with them. She noticed his eyes focus on the already powered-up craft.

"They've come for the batch of weapons," Zoe whispered to Pietro. "Hide yourself. I'll take care of this."

While Pietro crouched down with a series of grumbles, Zoe stepped out from the rows of craft onto the main concourse and headed toward the arriving troop delegation. Tarmun caught sight of her and waved her over. She walked up with a cautious gait, with the hope her story held, and they had no reason to check the ship that had just happened to be in standby mode.

Zoe gave a salute to Tarmun, who returned it after a moment. "Ready for the delivery?"

Tarmun's face twisted in a slight scowl. "It's the regular delivery time, so we're ready."

Zoe nodded hastily. "I've got your supplies ready in the back." She motioned down the hallway, but Tarmun paused.

"What were you doing with that starcraft over there?"

Zoe swallowed the knot in her throat. "This craft failed one of our final verification checks. It could be nothing, but I didn't want to release it until I make another pass, ensuring it's flight and combat ready."

Zoe prayed that bone was enough for Tarmun to be satisfied, but instead, he took a step toward the craft. "Looks in good shape to me. You know, we're gunning up for a run. I'm hearing about potential trackers in the far reach, and we could always use a fast ship to get us there."

"You don't want to trust that heap before we vet it, Captain." Zoe's tone had drifted into begging. She hoped Pietro hadn't set his sights on Tarmun and his group, which had all tabled Zoe's delivery for the moment and focused on the craft, its engines now in a partial burn, casting a glow in the far end of the cavernous room.

Tarmun's eyes narrowed into a glare; his voice sharpened to a bark. "Lt. Enix, I order you to transfer that starcraft to us now."

Zoe searched for reasons, excuses, and even unveiled threats that may have redirected Tarmun's attention away from the ship, but she realized it was hopeless, especially once Tarmun muttered, "Someone's aboard that ship right now."

Pietro was done hiding. Tarmun eyed Zoe with disbelief. "What the world is going on here?"

As Tarmun stepped past Zoe toward the craft, she felt panic take hold. The other Zamas troops nearby unshouldered their rifles.

"Wait!" Zoe shouted. Tarmun turned back to her. Zoe's mind raced for any kind of explanation that would've been remotely acceptable, but her extended pause was the worst possible non-answer she could've provided.

Tarmun pointed at Zoe. "What are you pulling here?" He slowly trained his rifle on her chest. "Whoever's on that ship, make them stand down now, or you'll be charred remains."

Zoe froze. It seemed that Pietro had gotten what he wanted and was ready to thrust her to her fate. She closed her eyes and hoped for warm thoughts of her sister as she begged a million times for mercy in her head. Several loud blasts came next. Zoe's body shook with the thundering reports, but she slowly realized she remained among the living. Soon after, she noticed the grunts and groans and opened her eyes to Tarmun and his group, laid out on the ground.

"Give me your hand!"

Pietro's voice howled above the engines as the craft was now overhead. Pietro himself was on the entrance ramp to the ship, extended downward a few feet from Zoe. Pietro reached for her with as much of a smile as Zoe had seen on his face since their first meeting.

She glanced back at her past and decided her future, however uncertain, had the best shot at revenge with Pietro and reached for his hand as their stolen starcraft made a hasty exit from Warehouse 13 and all of Cerulia.

Chapter Seven

SINCE THEIR ABRUPT DEPARTURE from Cerulia, Zoe remained in the navigator seat as Pietro skillfully guided the *Outspan* at a blistering speed into deep space. Zoe eyed the rear view of the craft on the ship console, where Cerulia rapidly grew smaller in the distance. Zoe was filled with many thoughts - regret certainly one of them. While she knew, in her heart, she needed to go after Malone, the other losses already adding up weren't anything she wanted. *What if one of those in the warehouse had been Quintus?* Just the thought drove a deep chill through Zoe. As a distraction, she eyed the flight controls of the *Outspan*.

Through her Retooling work, Zoe had become familiar enough with the general layout panels of starcraft, but it was quite different now that she was aboard one out in space. After a few moments of watching the various scopes and indicators, she turned back to Pietro. "It's so busy."

Pietro smiled. "Never seen a craft in actual flight before, I take it?"

"No. Back in the warehouse, I've fired up and tested components, but one at a time. Seeing the ship in full service, it's-"

Zoe still found herself unable to complete a thought, but she was mesmerized. The concert of alert tones and fluid energy the ship took on its own as it glided through space was a sight for her.

Pietro seemed at home at the ship's console and directed the *Outspan* on a steady arc toward the Far Reach area of Ling Galaxy.

"We must vanish for a bit to work out our plan," Pietro said. He glanced at Zoe with triumphant eyes over their successful impromptu heist. "That was fun, wasn't it?"

For the moment, Zoe had accepted her status as rescued from a close call. She shifted in her seat. "Not my idea, but I'll take being alive over what they had in mind." She lowered her head.

Pietro watched her with compassion. "It's ok. Yes, you're now an outcast. I've been one for a while now. I get what that's like. It hurts and can certainly be scary: being an unknown, all by yourself. This galaxy doesn't care for those who can't contribute."

" I had a place and a life back there, and I just threw it away. You were cast out. There's a difference." Zoe retorted.

Pietro set the *Outspan* on autopilot and leaned back with a deep inhale. Zoe had seen the look before. Pon had shown a similar expression. It usually happened before Pon launched into a speech about some greater good garbage like the rest of the politicians on Network did about any number of things. Those who died in famines, succumbed to Veculus, or converted to following Malone, were all part of some master plan to those in power, acceptable casualties in a process that most leaders claimed or at least acted like they were in control of while, in reality, none of them knew the next move. Their only play was recovering from the current predicament and keeping their core base happy come re-election time.

Pietro moved near Zoe. She glanced away, but he pulled her back to his eyes with his hand.

"Zoe, listen. The situation you're in, this whole galaxy is in, is because a few people decided it best they be in control. They don't care about your sister; they don't care about your people. Your government accepted this. I give them credit for that. But they've, in turn, forced their people into making things right. I believe all races have to have some stake in their future, but to declare your own race slaves until that happens is not only foolish, it's very destructive. How many of you are living for anything other than the next haul? There's no spirituality, no family, no growth. What do you have to offer Ling Galaxy in the end except for production? Believe me, the UA would enlist you all tomorrow, but you'd be no better. You can't live a life based on providence. There has to be more. That's what I'm doing. That's what I want to get out of this. If you'd stop and think, I'm the best hope for Ling Galaxy to thrive as it was always meant to."

Pietro made his way into the common forward area adjacent to the bridge. Several feet back, the corridor opened into a more flowing space with a table for plotting courses and other general work. After a few moments, Pietro called Zoe to join him.

"I'm going to try contacting Malone. I don't know if this will work, but it's worth a try. I want to see where his head is now."

"Is it a good idea to let him know you're around? Shouldn't we be more secretive?"

Pietro smiled. "Child, I won't be speaking with him. I'm only connecting with his being, seeing where he's located. We can track him on Network, and I have, but what I'm going to try here should give us his location, to the planet and even relative to his exact position. So, if we're going to get him, this is how."

While Pietro focused his body, Zoe did her best to hide a chuckle, figuring that was the last thing Pietro wanted to hear. But it was funny to her: the sight of Pietro's gyrations on the floor. She'd never been one for UA Mysticism. Zoe had lost enough family that it made the idea of some benevolent force watching over, guiding and, even more so, providing for them seem pretty ridiculous.

Zoe waited for Pietro's confirmation, but instead something caught his eye. For a second, Zoe wondered if she'd entered incorrect coordinates. "What is it? What's wrong?"

Zoe followed Pietro to the bridge console, where he pointed to a nearby quadrant on the navigation display. "It can't be."

Zoe looked at the mini display window Pietro had opened.

Aside from a few nearby asteroids and some random space debris, she saw an inconspicuous cargo ship escorted by a collection of UA fighters.

"Some kind of cargo transport; maybe a prisoner ship. I've seen a couple, partially dismantled, anyway. So, what's got you worried about it?"

Pietro clasped his chin, gazing at the convoy as if it were an ancient artifact he'd studied his entire life. Then, he jabbed a finger toward one of the other ships escorting the transport. "That ship is Nara class."

"Nara? I didn't think they traveled in Ling like that."

"They don't." Pietro finally glanced back at Zoe. "Not only is it Nara class, but that's the ship of the Hierarch. Ellene Ballo is in Ling."

"Who?"

"Leader of the Nara, child. It looks like our friend, Malone, has drawn Ellene Ballo into the fray."

The lift in Pietro's voice had Zoe wondering. Nara were typically unseen. She'd never even seen any until Pietro. The Nara's place in Ling were as deliverers of Essence. And, the ones who came to Ling weren't anything like leaders. But now, there were three: Pietro, Malone, and Ellene. Was the hunt for Essence that big of a threat they sent the Nara Hierarch into the mix?

Zoe was puzzled by Pietro's sudden shift about Ellene and why Pietro was distracted by her.

Zoe asked, "Can't we use Ellene to get Malone?"

Pietro shrugged. "She's certainly a game piece. I'm not interested in hitting Ellene right now, however. But, she could be useful to us."

The Nara starcraft shimmered much more brightly than the other ships around it. Its brilliant color shone as vividly as a jewel against the blackness around it.

"What's Ellene like?"

Pietro mulled the question over with a few muffled chuckles. Then, as he checked some of the shipboard monitors, he replied,

"Very particular. I'm surprised she's shown her face in Ling like this. It shows how desperate she is."

A series of loud explosions jolted Zoe out of her seat. The *Outspan* buffeted wildly, and several alarm notifications blared on the console.

"What was that?" Zoe asked as she climbed back into her chair.

"Oh, it's them," Pietro replied glumly. He tapped a control on the console and displayed the rearview, where two fighters were close and fixed on their ship.

"Who?" Zoe asked.

"Railen. It's fair to say they don't know who's on this ship. They just want it. They too were former Nara, cast out for their crimes. They spent years in Ling Galaxy surviving and now are out for recompense. Revenge against all. Retribution is their only creed. They don't care who and how. They just want to see everything burn."

Zoe grabbed the *Outspan's* controls and swung in an evasive move. "There's got to be something we can do here."

Pietro pounded his fist against the wall. "Nothing I'd like to."

Another series of blasts resounded, but these found their mark. The ship shuddered violently, and the console panel blinked off for a few moments, then back on, only to display several alerts.

"They've damaged our shields. We're not going to last much longer like this."

Zoe glanced at the proximity scan for any local systems they could duck down into. If they could at least remove themselves from the *Outspan*, they could survive, hoping the Railen just wanted to take fresh scrap.

When things seemed at their worst, and Zoe had yet again prepared herself for a reunion with her sister, another series of blasts sounded, but these were different. A new grouping of starcraft entered the scene. Zoe and Pietro watched as the new craft lit into their attackers until the Railen ships were obliterated in brilliant showers of light and debris.

Their ship comm crackled to life with a voice speaking a language Zoe didn't recognize. Thankfully, Pietro did.

"That's Omegan. Hit the translator, quick."

The jabber turned to intelligible speech. The voice through the Outspan comm was scratchy but deep. "Starcraft, identify yourself."

Pietro cleared his throat. "We are charges of Malone Stanton. We were on a mission to retrieve vital tech for his eminence when we were overrun."

Zoe noticed the mirthful look in Pietro's eye. For some reason, despite their attempted ruse and the prevailing fact the Omegans may not have even believed it, she felt a strange calm over their uncertain outcome. The comm was silent for a while, but then an answer came. "Carry on. Watch for stray Railen and UA ships. We may not be so close next time to assist."

"Understood, thank you. Hail Omegana."

"Hail Omegana," came the reply.

The Omegan craft zoomed away from the scene.

* * *

Zoe had known enough about the Omegans and their attitude towards anyone who wasn't. Some of the smashed and burned tech the Cerulaks recovered included Omegan parts, but those weren't as plentiful as the others. Omegans were known for their ruthlessness and also their fighting skill. It wasn't many a fight they lost, and even fewer they walked away from willingly.

"How did you do that?"

Pietro still looked out the front of the *Outspan* with a satisfied grin. "I guess I still have some abilities after all." He slowly turned and faced Zoe. "In addition to work I've done with Essence, I was a quick study in the field of mental grasp. It's an ancient technique only a few Nara have ever been able to learn. It's only taught to a select few in Nara Instruction, those determined to have the highest aptitudes."

"So, you fed them the idea of leaving us alone, and they went with it like that?"

"Yes. Exactly like that."

Zoe was amazed that Pietro openly admitted to commanding the minds of other beings with the cavalier approach of someone hauling containers of space scrap. Suddenly, she was afraid about who else Pietro may have tested or used his abilities on.

"So, is mind control how you got me to cooperate and get you this ship?"

Pietro's mouth formed a line, taking in a slow breath. Then, he stood and approached Zoe, his hands outward and his arms at his sides. "I can understand why you'd suspect that. The truth is, I've been adrift in this galaxy for some time, and it's been quite lonely. I know there's more to this life than just accomplishing something. I need to have people around me that I care about. That's exactly what Malone has done for himself. I can tell those people who are massing in his honor truly believe in what they've seen, even though you and I both know his real agenda is more sinister than his devoted acolytes care to admit."

Klaxon alerts sounded on the bridge, and several warnings flashed on the forward screen. Zoe ran some checks until her worst fear stared back at her from the console. "Pietro, the Regulator's been hit. We're not going to get far at all without fixing that. We've got to find a port or something. There's too much damage on these console indicators to ignore."

Pietro nodded. He then activated a map scan of the area and flicked his hand about, moving the display among the various moons and planets nearby. "Ahh, planet Bertold. It's got a port, and it's still under UA control, for some reason. So, let's head there, see if we can get some help."

Zoe toggled through the controls, and with Pietro's guidance, they angled the dinged, slightly smoking *Outspan* toward Bertold and a hopeful respite for repairs.

Chapter Eight

"**I**T'S SO BLUE!"

Zoe's eyes were fixed on the landscape as it cascaded past the forward viewport of their cruiser. Deep bluish oceans that looked to stretch to the horizon gave a stark backdrop to a series of islands that appeared occasionally. She caught Pietro's chuckle and glanced over at him.

"Pretty remarkable, isn't it? Bertold has been called the Well of Ling Galaxy for a good reason. There's plenty of industry here harvesting aquand for other planets which aren't as saturated," Pietro said.

A large collection of islands quickly passed below their ship. A collection of giant starcraft were positioned near one island, and she noticed large receptacles that scooped massive amounts of the bluish liquid into them.

"So that's where they get our Aquand."

"Good chance of that. But we're not here for a drink break."

Zoe's eyes met Pietro's. "Of course. The Regulator. This place looks pretty sparse on tech for repairs. Think we'll have any luck?"

Pietro shrugged. "Oh, I think we'll find something. Bertold has a few ports of record. We just have to find one with a decent market."

Pietro's confidence eased Zoe's concerns a bit. She figured Cerulia couldn't have been the only planet in Ling destitute enough from the Dark Times to have been in the scrapping field. So, Pietro guided the *Outspan* closer to an island cluster until their mostly aquatic foreground became a large plateau of dry land.

"Here we are. Kandam City."

Kandam City boasted a spaceport, trading market, and a series of smaller settlements. Pietro guided the *Outspan* to an open area near one of the markets, touching down for a mostly uneventful landing. As Zoe got up from her seat, she wondered what they would offer in trade for a new Regulator.

"Please tell me you've got a Wenzo crystal or two under those robes."

Pietro offered a mild glare in return. "No. But, for the resourceful, credit is unlimited."

Pietro headed toward the rear of the Outspan, his robes billowing behind him. After a moment of watching him exit and shaking her head at his flippant attitude, Zoe searched the *Outspan* for anything that could've helped them make a trade. Pietro was pretty confident, but even Zoe knew that in the real world of Ling, besides hard currency, items of value were the only true transaction method with any chance of success. *Outspan* had been readied for Cerulak Zamas use, so a series of troop arms were aboard. Zoe pulled out two long-range pulse rifles from storage compartments. The guns wouldn't have equaled to a Regulator, but it was a start. Next, she added a series of charge explosives and some rations to her haul. The pickings were slim, but Zoe felt better about having more to barter with than Pietro's attitude.

Zoe met Pietro outside as he surveyed the area and the trading market nearby. Feeling the weight of everything, Zoe plopped the case of rations and gently laid the charges down when she noticed Pietro looking at her.

"What is all that?"

"Currency. I don't know if you've ever done any trading. I haven't exactly, but I know the value of items. We're not going to get a Regulator for free. We have to give something in return."

"And you think you've got sufficient value in that pile?" Pietro added with a smirk.

"Maybe not, but it's a start. You have a better idea?"

"Child, I chose our landing spot because the trading markets are less patrolled by local security forces. Don't you think we could've just headed over to that spaceport and done some quick thievery, taking a Regulator off one of those ships and then making a break for it?"

Zoe eyed the port, where several cruisers stood, being fueled. "We wouldn't have gotten far. As sparse as the port is, I bet it's tightly monitored. Harvesting Aquand is a key industry in Ling, so they've probably got that locked up tight."

"You're astute and correct." Pietro strode about Zoe as she eyed him. "No, I've not come all this way to be picked up for simple tech theft. These trading markets give hope to so many in Ling Galaxy. We just have to wait for someone as needy as us to get here and grab what we need from them."

"And this stash?" Zoe nudged the rations container with her boot.

Pietro eyed the pile with mild pity. "Save the rations. Trade the weapons if you want to get more nourishment. But leave the explosives on board. Never know when those could come in handy."

Annoyed at Pietro's sparse sharing of information, Zoe yanked the ration packs into her arms and grabbed the explosives as gingerly as her annoyance would allow.

As she reached a free hand for a rifle, Pietro said, "Leave the weapons. I may have use for them after all."

Zoe looked into Pietro's eyes, wondering for a moment if he was joking. But, after he stayed silent, she replied, "This stuff isn't as light as it looks, by the way." She went back up the catwalk and wondered just what kind of situation she was in with Pietro. She felt more like an indentured servant than a partner in a revenge plot. Once she got back to the *Outspan* cargo hold, she tossed the ration pack onto a counter and laid the explosives behind one of the seats to the rear of the bridge. After a moment of pounding the counter near the rear cargo hold to bleed off excess aggravation, she returned outside and saw Pietro talking with an elderly Mardak. The short hairs on their body all had a bit of greyish tint. Zoe approached, and after a few moments, she caught Pietro's gaze. He extended a hand and beckoned her closer.

As Zoe neared, a noticeable stench invaded her nostrils. While she glanced around to see if a waste vehicle had come close by, she realized it was the Mardak.

Pietro smiled warmly at her. "Ah, glad you came back so quickly. Zoe Enix, I'd like you to meet Rezin Salko. Rezin is a retired member of the Aquand harvest teams on Bertold."

Rezin, amid a series of groans, straightened himself up. "Hello, Ms. Enix. I was telling your partner here I came into the markets to get some odds and ends for my return trip to Zormad. He asked me about the Aquand industry here on Bertold and that you two were looking for an investment?"

Zoe, unsure of Pietro's ruse, played along out of curiosity. "Yes, that's correct. We've been location scouting, and I've seen several harvesters around. Are there open areas not subject to claim?"

"Well, I can't say I'm the best versed in those matters, but I think you can check with the council on Bertold Island. It's roughly a two-hour flight from here, give or take the abilities of your craft."

Pietro laughed and patted Rezin's back. "Yes, of course. Thanks to the trading market, we'll hopefully get a few things for the rest of our stay here. Tell me, Rezin, would you care to have some dinner with us this evening?"

Rezin's face twisted with concern. "Oh, I don't know. I've been on Bertold longer than I expected. I really should be shoving off."

Pietro said, "Please, I insist! I can certainly make it worth your while somehow. I've got skill with these trading markets. I bet I can get you more items for your return home. Seeing the family, I take it?"

Rezin shuffled in place. Zoe still hadn't grasped Pietro's use of Rezin in their repair calamity, but she felt a little sorry for the elderly Mardak.

"Oh, I suppose the missus wouldn't mind another day's wait for my return. Provided you can get me some Bertolian fragrance or something?"

Pietro chuckled. "I can't imagine we couldn't find something along those lines. Zoe, I'm going to take Rezin to the market for some shopping. Why don't you join us?"

Zoe followed Pietro as he worked his way through the market with Rezin. It amazed Zoe how Pietro moved Rezin from cautious prey to willing participant in such a short time. After some beverages and a bit of trading, Pietro had managed to get a fairly impressive haul for Rezin and themselves. None of the items included a Regulator, however. By this stage, though, Zoe figured Pietro knew what he was doing. She only hoped whatever it was wasn't too rough on Rezin. He seemed pretty nice, if not a little out of sorts.

They found themselves behind Rezin's craft in the evening. Nights on Bertold proved to be of the chillier variety. Zoe wrapped her arms around her frame and edged closer to the torch pit. While primarily intended for meal preparations, the heat it generated came in handy on cold nights. Of course, staying warm wasn't exactly its intended purpose, but Zoe wasn't in the place or mood to complain about it, given how far she was from everything she knew.

Pietro had parlayed the gold trim on his robe for some Grondian Ale and had shared it with Rezin. The old Mardak had relaxed a bit, but Zoe was still on guard about the situation, despite Pietro not showing any malice.

Pietro held his cup high. "To the glory of Ling Galaxy. May she one day remember all the poor lost souls under her care and give them the treatment they all deserve."

"Snallack!" Rezin exclaimed as he lifted his cup in kind. Zoe eyed

Pietro quizzically, and Pietro shrugged. Then, after a moment, Rezin let loose with a belch and wiped his mouth. "Forgive me; sometimes I forget where I am and lapse into my native tongue."

"Not a problem, friend. Drink up!" Pietro guided the bottle to Rezin's cup for a refill.

"What are you doing?" Zoe hissed, but Pietro gave her a stern glare in response.

"You know, Rezin, if I'm not mistaken, your craft is of an older line in Ling Galaxy."

"That's correct, before the days of that Transient Warp business. Back when starcraft were tough, and they had what it took both for intergalactic travel and for a brawl now and then."

Zoe hadn't recognized the likes of Rezin's ship, which surprised her a bit. The tech she'd seen in Warehouse 13 seemed to be only so many years old, which made her wonder about the exact age of the strange ship.

Pietro, still engaging with Rezin, said, "Magnificent vessel. If I'm not mistaken, that had one of the earlier uses of the Hayes Targeting systems?"

"Oh, I'm not much of an old soldier. But Mardaks were always ready for a fight. We're not given a lot in Ling Galaxy we don't scrap for ourselves, you know."

Pietro nodded. "Your kind has been mistreated for a long while. There'll come a time for you. You'll get what you deserve, believe me."

Rezin leaned back in his seat, seemingly content. Zoe marveled at Pietro's way, and seeing Rezin's change over a brief period, from unsure to downright friendly with Pietro, had her wondering just how much of her change towards Pietro had been about the same thing. Zoe, like Rezin, wasn't exactly in a place of fulfillment, and she wanted so badly what Pietro seemed to magically fill or, at least, gave the strongest impression he could.

After another long swig of his drink, Pietro wiped his mouth and nodded toward Rezin's craft. "That's it. I can't take it anymore. I'm not going to get any peace until I look at that console of yours."

Rezin chuckled a bit. "You're pretty curious, aren't you? Ok, I suppose it's the least I can do after the company you've given me and the fragrance." After a few unsteady attempts, Rezin got to his feet and stumbled toward the craft. Pietro set his cup down and stepped back quickly to Zoe.

"Get ready for my signal - you'll need to pull that Regulator out once I'm done."

"Done with what?" Zoe hissed.

Pietro responded with a look that told Zoe so many things she feared. Unfortunately, her concerns about Rezin weren't unfounded, and her heart sank as she realized she was an accomplice to whatever Pietro had in store next.

Zoe followed them from behind and lingered inside the aft section of the craft as Pietro guided Rezin up slowly. The ale had worked a number on Rezin, so much so that Pietro needed to almost carry him through the corridors to the front of the ship.

Zoe looked around the hold section. It was stowed with a few unremarkable items. A store of rations for a return trip. Old and spent harvesting equipment that had a layer of grime on it, probably from some kind of land mining. She figured Rezin would've sold any aquatic mining equipment upon his retirement.

The dull hum of the onboard ship systems was the only sound Zoe heard for a while. Zoe wondered what the signal was when a klaxon buzz sounded over the comm, scaring her. The shrill alarm buzz came with Pietro's voice over the speakers.

"Zoe, harvest the Regulator. I'll be right down."

It took Zoe a few minutes to locate the access panel. It was different from other craft she'd worked on in the past, but the design of the engines, particularly the Regulator access, wasn't that much of a different layout. Without tools at her disposal, she was left to hand-loosen the connectors. Her hands were soon covered with a bit of grease, but she held a Regulator after some wrangling of latches. Finally, she slid out of the maintenance hatch to see Pietro, his robe decorated with grayish blood.

Zoe froze for a moment before speech found her. "What did you-"

"I did what was necessary for someone on a mission like ours. As did you."

Pietro grabbed the Regulator from Zoe's hands and walked past her. "Come now. It's time we get back to our mission. The sooner we get Malone, the better."

Zoe weakly followed in silence. The sooner the better was right, but the rising body count on this quest had become harder and harder for her to stomach.

* * *

As they returned to space, Zoe was anything but settled in her seat. The thought of Rezin and whatever Pietro had done to him was a tough visual to shake. Even though she hadn't seen whatever Pietro did, the idea of that kindly old Mardak being killed just for their mission weighed on her. She did her best to push the feelings down and thought back to why she was going along with this in the first place.

"Pietro, you didn't have to kill Rezin, did you? So why did you bother giving him the ale, making friends with him, the whole lead on?"

Grief tore at Zoe. She hadn't even known of Rezin's existence hours earlier, but the feeling of his death partly from her cooperation with Pietro stung her deeply. "I don't understand why you couldn't have just stolen it from another craft or even stolen it from his."

"It's simple, child. I had to show you what commitment is. You've been committed to a life on your former world. What has that given you? Safety, security, a purpose, a value. You're someone because you believed in that cause. But now you've got another desire in your heart. Your service to your beloved country isn't enough anymore. You want to kill, but you're not a rabid animal in the street. You're an intelligent being, capable of things, but maybe not yet of murder. But now, you see what it takes. You've committed yourself to a cause without thinking of the depth of what your desire is. Murdering one of the most notorious beings in Ling Galaxy isn't the fodder for a child's playtime. The level of depravity needed to kill Malone Stanton means you must also be relentless. You must stop at nothing, including stealing from a kindly old soul like poor Rezin. Just think of how sad his family will be to find out about his murder at the hands of a mysterious assailant. We were removed from the municipality of Kandam City and their UA delegation. The trading markets are where the real economy of Ling Galaxy resides. And that economy allows for the appropriation of resources to the quick and the determined. That's what we are, and for the greater good of relieving Ling Galaxy of its greatest enemy, a few poor souls killed as collateral damage are more than acceptable. So, ask yourself, Zoe Enix, just how far are you committed to your goal?"

"Where are we headed now?" Zoe asked, her eyes looking out the front canopy into deep space.

Pietro returned to the navigation console and tapped out several calculations. "We need a play. We're alone and not very formidable. I can't match Malone by myself. He's got too much on his side. So, I'm going to develop a play against his weakness, and when the time comes, we'll use that very soft spot to crush him. We'll be hiring someone for our plan," Pietro muttered. "Someone with skill. A smuggler should work fine."

"Why do you need someone else? I thought you had skills enough to go after Malone."

Pietro smiled at her. "Glad you've recognized that. But, truthfully, the hire isn't for direct attack. This is part of my plan; truthfully, there's one smuggler I need to get the job done. However, luring that party in will take some work. I've tracked him around Ling Galaxy. Our party has a few ties to planet Wenzo. So, it's a safe wager he'll be back there at some point."

"Mmhmm." Zoe leaned back into her seat. She'd been on the go so much she hadn't realized how exhausted she was but was quickly reminded, and felt her eyelids go heavy. Finally, she drifted off to sleep with the sound of Pietro's voice mentioning a planet called Wenzo.

* * *

As Pietro brought the *Outspan* into the skies over Wenzo, Zoe eyed the swiftly approaching port and clutched the pulse pistol. After landing, they headed for the town of Marwen. Zoe observed the area's inhabitants, as much as the scattered rabble of shabbily dressed individuals would've counted as the citizenry of any organized nation.

Zoe followed Pietro until they were across from the Dark Passage bar. The exterior was a mangled mixture of girders, likely former building pieces, twisted into an industrial-themed marquee that screamed a lot of things about the bar, none of which were overly friendly. The bar's title was emblazoned in shiny gray letters amid the blackish woven metal pattern. It would've been pretty acceptable as a prison entrance were there not bar grub and libations for sale.

"Are you really going in there?" asked Zoe.

"Of course."

"What exactly in there helps us to get Malone Stanton?"

"Because, my dear, now that you've had a lesson in commitment, you must learn approach. We can't run a search for Malone in a straight line. He's far too cunning not to see that coming. So, we'll do the next best thing - the trackers that can locate him. I'm going to look for soldiers for hire here. These bars are good for a few things, like a night's pleasure and a reliable mercenary."

That was enough for Zoe. She could've used more time, preferably with some strong drink, to further drown the image of Rezin's blood on Pietro's cloak. Once Pietro headed towards the bar, Zoe lost herself for a few moments in the scene inside. She hadn't been in any places like this, even on Cerulia, in her life. Cerulaks weren't much for frivolity past a young age and usually immersed themselves in work. Places like the Dark Passage weren't usual topics of discussion for them.

A group of bulky-looking beasts squeezed past Zoe and Pietro into the bar. They wore medium-grade armor and looked to be warriors of some kind. Pietro nodded in their direction. "Soldiers for hire. See, we're in the right place. I won't waste my time dealing with them one-on-one, though."

The hulking creatures looked like they could've mangled just about anyone they wanted to with their bare hands. "Why not grab one of them, give them a talk, and we get moving?" Zoe asked.

Pietro shook his head while his eyes darted around. "Places like these usually have a broker. I'm starting at the top. I suggest you stay close and don't make eye contact. Stand near but not too close to me. As I said earlier, the reasons for coming to this place are pretty simple: looking for work, looking for a fight, or looking for physical gratification."

Zoe narrowed her eyes and glanced back around the dimly lit room. A long bar divided the area pretty evenly with a few empty spots. She headed for a seat along the bar and saw Pietro follow suit.

After they sat for a few moments, a blonde female bartender came by. She had the world-weary look of someone who'd spent too many hours working in a place like the Dark Passage and was every bit aware of that fact. However, the sight of Pietro melted the barkeep's calm facade a bit into one of blunt surprise. "Um, hi?"

Pietro nodded. "Greetings. I won't waste your time with idle chatter, and I can already tell my appearance has you wondering just who or what I am. Believe me when I say that's none of your concern, and you shouldn't worry about finding out. Understand?"

The barkeep nodded.

"What's your name?" Pietro asked coolly.

The bartender blinked as she attempted to regain her composure. "Dian."

"Wonderful. Dian, I understand this is a great place to hire individuals for work, for various trades."

"It can be." Dian glanced downward, pretending to wipe the bar.

Pietro nodded. "Relax. Keep up your charade. It's best for you anyway. What I'm offering in payment is probably higher than most of your average clients would even consider."

Dian's eyes darted about behind Pietro. "Mmhmm."

"I'm looking for Railen trackers." Pietro had lowered his voice a tad, as even he knew the seriousness of that kind of request.

That brought Dian's eyes slowly back to his. "Railen-"

"-Trackers, that's correct. Now listen. I've got two million in Wenzo Crystals for whoever can deliver one to me."

Dian's eyes widened a bit. She glanced around before she leaned in closer to Pietro, lowering her voice. "We've got a lot of smuggler play in here. I can't rightly say who the best is. I mean, that kinda thing is more about personal preference, who's less of a dick, who's messier about the jobs, things like that."

"I'm sure you have your ways of doling out the work. I'm not going to leave the usual coordination to you, though. This is too serious a run for me to do that, but I'm fine with you passing the word around. I trust you know what I'm talking about and how serious it is."

Dian nodded. "Yep. But you know, I'd feel a lot better about asking around if I knew there was some take in it for me."

Pietro seized up a bit. Zoe noticed Pietro's back heaved more with several sharp breaths.

Finally, Pietro responded. "I can give you five hundred UA credits for your trouble."

Dian nodded. "I'll see who I can rustle up."

Pietro nodded. "Good enough. Give me something to leave a contact channel. Do me a favor and give this out only to someone who is up to the task. Remember, I found this place and you. Don't think I can't return just as easily and be a serious problem for you."

Dian slid a bar register and marker to Pietro while she continued her spree of pretend cleaning. Pietro grabbed the implements, and after a moment's pause, he wrote while a devious grin formed on his face.

Pietro slid the finished note back to Dian and patted the bar gently. Dian seemed relieved. "Are you having a drink or anything?"

Pietro stood. "No, that will be quite enough."

Dian quickly nodded as she pulled off the page with Pietro's note and slid it into her pants pocket. "Ok, then I guess that's all."

Zoe and Pietro headed out of the Dark Passage. She'd thought the visit would've cleared things up about Pietro's search, but they'd only added more questions and mysteries. *Why was Pietro willing to hire someone to find the Trackers? Why had he risked exposing himself in a public place like that?*

"Stop right there," Zoe commanded Pietro as he prepared to move them back to their ship.

Pietro lingered in his stance and eyed Zoe for a few moments before he relaxed and stood upright. "What?"

Zoe flung her arms upwards. "What? Oh, I don't know. Suppose you tell me more about what you're doing here. I helped you get that ship because you told me - no, you promised me - that you'd bring me to Malone. But so far, all we've done is kill some of my people, a Mardak, and go to a tavern attempting to hire someone to find Trackers. We're nowhere nearer to Malone than before we began, and I wonder if I haven't made a mistake coming all this way with you."

At first, Pietro looked at Zoe with annoyance, but then a smidgen of compassion blended in. "I sometimes forget what it was like to be the betrayed one, the one with the ideas that someone else took over when I hadn't the control I thought I did. Let me explain. I want to get Malone to corner himself, and this is the best way to do that."

"Well, what will hiring some random soldier get us?"

"We're not hiring a random soldier - we're aiming to get Malone's son to find a Railen Tracker, so we can kidnap him and use him to draw Malone to us."

Chapter Nine

BACK IN HER SEAT, ZOE'S MIND wandered again. Plenty had happened in just over a day, and she wasn't sure about any of it. Her path had become as jagged and uncertain as it ever was.

Pietro's take on the Trackers at least made more sense than their previous capers. She accepted they needed the Regulator for a workable craft, but the death of Rezin was a breach. Didn't others deserve their piece of happiness too? And, what was happiness for Zoe if it meant someone else died for it?

A proximity alert sounded on the console. Zoe adjusted the scan and zoomed in on a convoy passing. She recognized the Nara craft from earlier. *Their ships look so pristine,* Zoe thought. *I wonder what one of those would fetch on a trading market?*

She showed the convoy to Pietro. After a few moments of studying it, he waved his hand. "She'll be in our sights soon enough. We must remain focused on the true prize."

Zoe tapped Network and accessed several feeds of updates from the planets across Ling. Multiple stories cascaded down the holographic display. She grabbed several that showed groups wearing some sort of ceremonial robes.

"Is that some kind of religion, like UA Mysticism?" Zoe asked.

Pietro eyed her with a grim look. "Oh, it's Mysticism, but more like the church of Malone. Those robes are a nod to ceremonial Nara garb, but they've been bastardized with Malone's mark. He's setting himself up as a prophet. If he keeps this up, he won't have to fire a shot. His people will take over Ling Galaxy for him."

The growing admiration for Malone worried Zoe regarding her plans. The blossoming support for Malone surely meant more people were willing to stand in the way of anyone who came after him, and she appreciated more and more Pietro's idea of a subtle approach to take Malone out of the picture.

Zoe expanded the report on Network, and she and Pietro watched the briefing together. The story explained Malone's doings on Agmon. Because he'd had so much success there, he decided to carry it on and head to planet Tausian, where Malone not only provided relief to a starving community but he took up residence with them. His move wasn't just to win over people and leave them to succeed or starve on their own. Instead, he remained for a time in a place, and his residence at Tausian had seen a legion of followers spring up, who erected shrines and temples to him.

"The Tillians have been starving for a while, like the Cerulaks. Can't imagine how bad off they are if they even considered following Malone." Zoe muttered.

She glanced at Pietro, who studied the report on screen intently. "We're not going to get too close to him unless we draw him out."

Zoe looked at the video of followers and wondered just how much Malone had a hand in Network and dictating the course of what was shown to the galaxy.

"They must've seen the slaughters, the murders he's committed, right?" Zoe turned to Pietro. "How can they deify him when he's a murdering bastard?"

Pietro shrugged. "It doesn't matter what the truth is if you can create a reality that sufficient people believe in." Then, with a mild chuckle, Pietro added, "I sense the snare we set on Wenzo is about to be sprung."

"Now then," Pietro paced, his arms folded behind his back. "I need to have the comm unit on this ship ready for when our prey from Wenzo takes the bait. Angle the ship in line with the nearest large star cluster. I want to make sure the reception is perfect."

Zoe worked with the controls for several minutes until the ship's pitch and yaw thrusters responded. Adjustments still took her some time. Pietro soon joined her and verified the *Outspan's* position was suitable for his comm contact.

"Keep an eye on that signal monitor. You'll see it adjusting, for better or worse, depending on your alignment." Pietro glanced out of one of the side views while Zoe kept working her controls.

Zoe jumped a bit when Pietro grabbed her shoulder.

"There, that's it!"

Zoe looked toward the end of Pietro's gnarled extended finger to a ring of stars arranged in an oval.

"Point the ship there."

Several more angling attempts passed, but then their craft was aligned.

"How are we supposed to know he'll be calling?"

"Remember, child; I can search minds. This individual wants a great deal, and the bait we left for him is too good to pass up."

Once the *Outspan* was proximally aligned for comm contact, Zoe set the ship to auto mode. She eased herself out of her seat and pulled into a full-body stretch. Her time spent working in the retooling factory hadn't left her much chance for lounging around, and the excessive amount of sitting she'd done in just a short while on the *Outspan* had taken a toll with a series of sharp pains along her back and legs.

She strode back to where Pietro sat near the Comm portal and launched into a routine of standing stretches. She gasped in mild discomfort as she felt her limbs slowly work their way back into being fully stretched. She later noticed Pietro watching her, a curious glint in his eyes.

"Something on your mind?"

Pietro quickly blinked and shuddered. "Hmm? Oh, no, I was just thinking about how we'll intercept Malone when the time comes."

"I still don't understand why we didn't go after Ellene Ballo. If she's who you say she is, I can't think of a better target to have Malone gun for."

"The problem with Ellene," Pietro countered, "is she'll likely have more than a few defenses with her that we won't be able to beat. All she'd have to do is have some Essence handy, and she could reduce this craft and everything in it, especially the two of us, to a lovely bit of space vapor."

"Well, doesn't Malone have the same ability?"

"Maybe. But Ellene having Essence is a certainty, especially if she's ventured into Ling. I'm not sure of how many Essence powers Malone has yet. Based on his stunt on Agmon, he's got the growth potential of Essence harnessed."

"Have you ever held Essence the way Malone has?"

The question startled Pietro. He glanced sideways, a pained look on his face. Zoe wondered just what had happened to him. The fact that he'd first realized the concept of harnessing Essence made her wonder just how he knew it was possible.

"I have been able to, but since they altered me like this, I don't know if it is possible anymore."

"Well, Malone did it, and wasn't he altered?"

"Yes, but he also had something I didn't: charisma. He developed an industry around himself, finding hope for the lost and discarded in Ling. I imagine he assembled a team, probably including other disconnected Nara, and worked out at least a few of our post-exile physical kinks. People talk about the Syndicate, but Malone's Network is far more dangerous. Their members aren't out for the quick pay and making a living, however devious it is. No. Malone's crew is in it for belief. And belief in a cause, especially a very destructive one, is one of the most powerful forces out there."

Zoe felt a very uneasy feeling throughout her body at Pietro's words, coupled with the wild look in his eyes. For the first time since she had learned about Zaratha's demise, Zoe wondered if the journey of retribution she'd been on was one she had the stomach for after all.

After a long moment at the comm with no incoming transmissions, Pietro rose and headed away for more meditation. While Pietro continued his chants, Zoe retreated to the rear of the Outspan. The comm station called to her. She'd been gone from Cerulia long enough. Maybe she was too far off from ever returning home. But the loneliness she'd felt, briefly absent while with Pietro, was back again. While she knew being back in Cerulia was probably a very doubtful option, she at least needed to grasp for a piece of home, something and preferably someone with whom she could talk. She tapped in the access code to contact Quintus. The comm cycled through the connection routine for a few moments, and then she heard a voice twisted in disbelief.

"Is that really you?"

Quintus appeared on the screen. His face was ashen. Aside from the dirt marks, his eyes said most of what Zoe had been feeling. "Zoe, what's going on? Are you ok?"

Zoe bit her lip and touched the screen. Her throat clenched, but she was too happy to keep quiet, no matter how shaky the words came out. "Hi, yes, I'm fine."

"There's been a major lockdown at Warehouse 13. I heard about a craft theft, and you'd been reported missing."

Zoe strained herself. She wanted to tell Quintus everything so much - that it wasn't her fault, that Pietro had overpowered her. But, the truth was, she'd been so focused on her path that she hadn't realized all that it may have cost her.

"Quintus, I've made an ally. Someone who can help me with what I've been wanting."

For a moment, Zoe thought the connection was broken, but no, it was Quintus frozen at the idea that Zoe's disappearance wasn't out of her control. Zoe saw in Quintus' eyes, the piecing together of precisely what may have happened at the Warehouse on Cerulia.

"Zoe, did you kill those Zamas soldiers?"

Her sides went taut. Quintus eyed her with widened eyes in silence. His question hung in the air between them.

"Not exactly."

Quintus' eyes winced; his mouth was agape. "Not... exactly."

The hope in Quintus' eyes slowly faded, and Zoe's happiness at seeing her old friend quickly jumped to desperation. She realized, at that moment, the friendship between them was at the very least tarnished, if not fractured beyond repair. Zoe's belief that a conversation with Quintus was the cure for all she'd missed was tossed out. Still, she was anxious for him to understand her. Quintus had to have known. He knew what she'd been through, what she'd been going through.

"You have to understand, Quintus. There was no other way."

Quintus bowed his head. "You're one of my oldest friends, Zoe. This is bad. Whatever you...you shouldn't have done this."

The truth in Quintus' words stung Zoe deeply. She knew he was right, but equally as much, she felt trapped in her current course - a path chosen for her that diverged from the rest of her former world.

"Are you going to tell anyone?"

"How could I not? Isn't that what you would've done? What happened to you? What happened to my friend?"

Quintus said no more. Zoe's body shook as she cried out, "I had to. There was no other way."

But the screen went black. Zoe's last tie to her people was gone. So, what was left for her? Blind vengeance?

* * *

Soon after Zoe's last call to Quintus, Pietro's mark took the bait. As Pietro assessed, Malone had been drawn out of hiding. Zoe had drifted into a fitful sleep after her painful conversation with Quintus, desperate to find the way back to her old self that her trip so far had destroyed.

"It's him!"

Pietro's explosive statement jolted Zoe awake. He was at the fore of the *Outspan*, his body bathed in the amber light of the map display, and one planet in particular was zoomed in so much it took up most of the screen.

After a few moments, Zoe stood and approached Pietro as she wiped her eyes. "Planet Tausian?"

"Yes, of course!" Pietro glanced at Zoe before he looked back at the map display. "How could I have missed it? Tausian was always a center of production in Ling, even before the Dark Times. Their distribution of Essence was always a shade higher than the other planets. The level of Replication they are capable of couldn't have been centralized, as it was deemed too volatile. As much as he needs control over Ling Galaxy, he has to have a hand on Replication. With the other planets like your home world being rendered useless, that makes Tausian an absolute gem of a target for him. See here; the UA has been staging craft nearby. This has to be it!"

* * *

While Tausian had once boasted a replication center, the native population of the planet hadn't appeared to have embraced or even benefited from the massive production environment. Zoe wondered if she'd made a mistake on the scans of the planet's population of Tillians, but it seemed that about twenty-five percent were organized in highly industrialized areas. She recognized the Replication layout, as many of the ruins on Cerulia dealt with abandoned Replication facilities. But, aside from the very metropolitan locations, there was a much more significant portion of the planet that consisted of a series of tented cities and what looked to be farming areas. Still, every one she viewed seemed overgrown, even covered over with sand, partially or entirely. She'd only heard about how the Tillians lived before then, but somehow she always imagined it to be different.

"Replication is the key to Malone's future," Pietro explained. "I know your world hosted a Replication industry for a while, so I won't bother with the details. But Essence, now that he's able to wield it, he'll have to reproduce it to become the supplier the Nara used to be and eventually turn his aim to eliminating Grondia. The well-intentioned but clueless lot the UA has been amassing their forces. A working Replication center is far easier to start with than the derelict remnants on your home world and the rest of the Far Reach planets. Malone will eventually head there, I'm sure of it. We just have to be near when the time comes and hope the snare we've set with his son takes effect and draws Malone out of his protective area."

Zoe looked back at the screen, and a deep ache hit her gut at something in the view of the area. She zoomed in closely on an object. It stood out from the drab background around it. The more she zoomed in, the faster her pulse beat in her throat until she recognized the person. The helmet and cape had been all over Network. The outfit of not just a warrior or a conqueror, but someone who claimed themselves to be the savior of Ling Galaxy himself.

"It's Malone. Pietro, look!"

Chapter Ten

ONCE ZOE OVERCAME THE SHOCK of seeing Malone in person for the first time, other emotions quickly took hold. She'd wanted this, dreamed of this, needed this for so long. She'd often wondered if it was even possible. Then, finally, Pietro made it happen for her. Pon Ebnora, with all her influence and power, couldn't even make this happen.

Zoe stared at the readouts of the *Outspan's* area scan in disbelief. "I thought Tausian was an advanced, developed planet. The Tillians who live here, they helped us rebuild Cerulia. They're technically gifted. Why are they living like this?"

Pietro glanced at the readouts and shrugged. "Prosperity isn't very contagious. Tillians clung to their simpler ways and chose a life away from the chains of technology and progress. It gave them a simpler life but also made some struggles of theirs tougher than others. There was a largely rural population of Tausian, as in many areas of Ling Galaxy. They supported their side of the world with crop production and fed the industrialized portion. But the famines hit them, like many others. Coupled with Veculus, it drove the once proud community into survival mode, much like your home planet."

Tears formed in Zoe's eyes as she watched the groupings of Tillians and heard Pietro's ongoing assessment of them. He talked about their deaths from starvation with the ease of someone reading assembly instructions. What hurt Zoe most was how much these poor, needy creatures gave their knowledge so freely to Cerulia when they themselves had next to nothing.

"What could Malone possibly want with them? They're no threat at all!"

"Spectacle, child. He wants spectacle. At this point, Malone can travel into a black hole, and he wouldn't be alone. Network would follow him. He's too well known to be ignored. He's caused enough of a stir in Ling Galaxy that any deed he does is captured. His Lookers, remember, disrupt whatever Malone doesn't want the galaxy to see, so the image of Malone to the masses remains a benevolent providing figure. He's winning this war through diplomacy, which is the best weapon available."

Zoe guided the *Outspan* on a mildly wobbling arc toward the settlement while she strained her eyes for a closer look. She hadn't made readouts of any substantial tech in the area, but there were plenty of life forms. Her Cerulak blood, long cooled from her endless mantra of revenge, suddenly found a new chill point as she realized what she was looking at.

"These are refugees at best, Pietro." Among the many casualties of the conflict in Ling Galaxy, the group before them was from another place, or maybe several. They were hunkered down and braced the best they could for something that may hit them or not. Uncertainty was just one of several unpleasant rules by which they lived. And Malone, the noble and decent one, had seen fit to take shelter among them.

"He's hiding in plain sight, using those Tillians as shields for himself. It's the basest of acts I could've ever expected from someone as ruthless as he is. See? He doesn't care about life; we've got to end his."

Zoe stared, motionless and silent. She heard Pietro's assessment, and whether he admitted it or not, Pietro had a philosophy that wasn't that far removed from Malone's. And suddenly, Zoe felt physically out of her body and watching the scene from somewhere else, from someone else's mind, from the sense of a sister watching her flesh and blood killed by Malone. *They're both in this,* she thought. *The less I do about this, the more I'm involved. It's not right to have anyone suffer.*

Zoe realized that what she wanted, what she needed, that she believed more than anything would've brought her peace, would, in this case, only further the cycle, creating more suffering in those left behind. *I can't stop them, but I can stop him.*

Zoe grabbed for Pietro's arm, and after a moment, he turned. But the look in his eye had changed. It wasn't the kindly supporting glance she'd seen. This had a far different glint.

"We're going to kill everyone down there."

"What?"

"Those are Malone's people. We must take them out. There's no telling how much he's infected them already."

"Pietro, these are Tillians. They aren't serving Malone. I know this for a fact. If anything, they are being held hostage."

Pietro replied with a silent glare.

"They are one of the few friends Cerulia has. I can't do it!"

Zoe shook at the realization that Pietro's vision wasn't so much for ending Malone but for becoming something similar himself. It was bad enough thinking of the deaths of her fellow Cerulaks in Warehouse 13 and kindly old Rezin. The murder of the Tillians, a race that had only offered Cerulaks comradeship, something her parents supported, was too much. Even her sister, Zaratha, couldn't have supported that. Zoe knew, no matter what, while she wanted Malone dead, furthering the trail of blood Pietro began only moved her down a path of becoming like Pietro, or worse yet, Malone.

I let Quintus down. I let Pon down. If I don't stop Pietro now, I'll let my parents and Zaratha down. And that I won't do.

"That's an unarmed settlement, Pietro." Still, Zoe tried to reason with Pietro over how killing even more innocents wasn't the right way to get Malone. Zoe glanced into Pietro's cold eyes, and a chill hit her body at the lack of remorse she found in them.

"N-no, we can't take out those Tillians."

"I'm not concerned with saving a few pathetic life forms. Don't you realize who that is? We'll lose our chance if we don't attack him now."

Zoe held onto her desire for revenge against Malone for so long, but she hadn't thought about what that revenge would've looked like. *What are we really doing here?* She wondered. *Any one of them down there could've been Zaratha. Am I any better for being part of their deaths than Malone was for killing Zaratha?*

The question asked, the answer was in front of her too, but she had ignored it. But now, it slapped her like a deluge of ice-cold water. The vengeance that had infected her soul, her entire being, had been revealed to be toxic. This wasn't her. This wasn't the sister Zaratha remembered, and it sure wasn't who Zaratha would've wanted alive, carrying on her memory.

Pietro shouted. "The weapons on this ship will easily lay waste to those people. Malone won't have time to fight back. What's the matter? From the moment I knew about you, I've known the desire that burns in your heart. I've given you what you've been wanting, haven't I? Now, do as I say and finish this!"

Pietro's eyes glowed a brilliant deep blue, and Zoe felt the anger that coursed out of his body. It wasn't hard to notice. He frightened her on their first meeting, but here he'd become scarier than she could've imagined. *Will that be me?* She wondered. *Will this rage consume me to that point one day? It can't. Zaratha wouldn't have wanted that.*

Zoe watched the Tillians surrounding Malone. Young males and females. Families. Babies. She squeezed the control yoke until her hands burned like fire. Her insides tensed until she shook.

Then, Zoe jerked her body to the left. The *Outspan* rolled

sharply in response until they were aimed at one of the nearest mountains.

Zoe looked into Pietro's wild eyes.

"I'm not helping you kill any more innocents."

"Not even innocents surrounding Malone Stanton?"

Zoe shook her head. "When we first met, and I told you about Malone Stanton, you said we'd only kill him. I'm not killing anyone that doesn't deserve it. My sister didn't deserve it, and neither do they."

Pietro frowned deeply. "This is our cause. Malone will kill far more than the few you see there, child. Don't think you're saving the galaxy by just protecting a few."

Zoe's path of revenge had taken her through the depths of her anguish and had driven a wedge between her and her people, even friends like Quintus, forever. It cost her so much, but with her life, she knew the enemy she was after had been hidden from her. It wasn't Malone but those who believed as he did. Pietro, as noble as he portrayed himself to be, was nothing more than another Malone, and while Zoe couldn't have killed Malone, she had in her reach the ability to at least stop someone who looked to be just as evil. Had she let Pietro kill Malone, what would Pietro have become? Another tyrant to one day decide another Zaratha was out of line enough to deserve being killed?

Zoe quickly hit the controls for a quick path out of the area, but Pietro slammed his fist on the console. She jumped and yelped in fright.

"Don't even think of that. We're finishing this, and you're going to help me. Don't you want this? This man killed your blood. It's time for revenge."

Pietro had so many gifts and abilities, but Zoe realized he was missing one thing that she still had. Connection to a family. She missed them, and it was too late to go back. But, she still had a play... one chance where what she did could've at least honored what her parents believed. So, with a steady hand, Zoe swung the *Outspan* around. Pietro stumbled about the bridge and clutched the walls for support.

"What are you doing?" Pietro's eyes glowed with a near neon tint.

"I can't stop you from doing what you want, but I can stop myself from helping you."

Alarms rang on the Outspan's onboard system as it veered on a beeline course for the nearest mountain ridge. Pietro, pinned down by the shift in g force, growled at Zoe, his voice twisted into a vibrating screech. "Stop now!"

But Zoe didn't. She felt more like herself and Zaratha's sister than she had since her fateful meeting in the Warehouse. She wasn't sure if this was the end, but she was ready for it if it was. Finally, her thoughts and conscience were clear.

400 METERS TO IMPACT.

Thoughts of Malone dimmed. *Malone won't get what's coming to him from me, but he'll get something someday. Someone will show him, to keep him under control, make him know what he stood for was nothing that Ling Galaxy wanted or ever needed.*

250 METERS TO IMPACT

Zoe grasped the controls so tightly her hands burned. She felt a hand on her shoulder and leaned forward, but Pietro's hands began to snake down her arms in an attempt to free them from the controls.

100 METERS TO IMPACT

He won't get me.

He won't reach me.

He's failed.

This is for you, Zaratha.

I love you.

In her final moments, Zoe felt a euphoric rush as years of pain over her losses and the pure hatred she felt over Malone whispered out of her system like an expelled infection. She cried tears of relief and joy as her surroundings were engulfed in white light and fierce heat.

The *Outspan* met the unremarkable mountain on Tausian in a

spectacular explosion. The fuselage of the Outspan was smashed in an instant into a small cube. Pietro had held onto a lever for the release hatch on the top, which broke free on impact, ejecting Pietro along with it.

* * *

Pietro woke in a daze. His vision blurred; he rubbed his eyes for an instant until the searing pain in his hand was too much, and he bellowed in agony. He raised himself slowly to a seated position. The ground beneath him was brittle, coarse, and dry. Through his clouded sight, he still made out the column of black smoke that wafted from where the *Outspan* had impacted and exploded into a million fragments, taking with it the only individual in Ling Galaxy who'd helped him at all.

His mind stirred at the sight and the thought of Zoe gone, and he was filled with confusion and anger. *How could she have done that?* He wondered. *I could've helped her. Unfortunately, she was too selfish to see it.*

Pietro staggered to his feet. His cloak and clothing were in tatters, and from the look of the ever-growing cloud of smoke from the crash site, he was stranded on the planet indefinitely. Finally, after a few hours' walk, he reached the settlement of Tillians he'd spotted previously. Although the collection of tented abodes was anything but advanced or even tech-heavy, Pietro knew, in time and some personal investment, opportunities were possible, even from the most unlikely of places.

Once the Tillians nearby caught sight of Pietro, they huddled and gave loud whoops. The cries were intent on scaring Pietro, but he strolled, his hands in the air.

"I come in peace," he spoke slowly. "I was a prisoner who escaped. My captors crashed that ship on your planet. I offer you my sorrow and hope to make reparations."

Pietro stood a good two to three feet taller than the Tillians.

Their small builds were nonetheless stocky. As Pietro moved, they edged closer to him in curiosity.

One of the Tillians, the tallest one of the group, approached Pietro. The cloaks that covered them were adorned with a ceremonial-looking hat. After a slight bow, they started. "We are a simple people. We don't tolerate aggression. If that's your cause, leave us in peace."

Pietro offered a slight bow in response. "I assure you, that's not my intent." He glanced around but saw no one around who hadn't appeared Tillian. "Tell me. I was looking for a Malone Stanton. Do any of you know where I might find him?"

The cloaked Tillian cleared his throat. "He transported off this planet. Said he had preparations to make."

Pietro gnashed his jaw. *Interesting move there, old friend. This chase of mine will continue later.* Then, nodding, he said to the Tillian chief, "Would you be so kind as to shelter me until I can arrange a way to get back to my people."

Pietro's offer was cautiously accepted. He was thankful the charm he'd developed during his exile from Grondia had taken hold, at least somewhat. He had to figure his way off-world from this place, however. The nearest craft available wasn't too close, and the meager abilities of the Tillians to communicate with the outside world were a significant problem for him. Still, he realized the isolation he once again found himself in was a little like his initial exile from Grondia. And, while that was a long road to pass, he had made it through that and had confidence he'd find his way back again somehow. However, Malone was still in his sights and wasn't ready to let that go.

Pietro crouched in the tent as the viewscreen blinked to life, and the picture changed to Pon Ebnora as she addressed her people on Cerulia. They'd reached another benchmark, and their forces had become strong enough for a more forward push into Ling Galaxy. No longer were they going to be the punching bag of the galaxy and cast aside by the more deliberate and powerful Omegans or even the resurgent Railen. The Cerulaks were ready to stake their claim in the galaxy.

"Good," Pietro thought. "More recruitment opportunities."

He believed to his core it was not only possible for him to continue, but his ordained destiny. He pulled the bowl of soup close and inhaled the fragrance of the spices for a moment before he hungrily devoured the warm liquid. It wasn't great, but like so much he'd done to get to where he was, it was enough.

STRATAGEM AWAKENING

Chapter One

"CAREFUL WITH THOSE MEASUREMENTS." Charista Mantisword nodded at the order from Bezar Hornell, her shift commander. Charista had checked the calculations on the navigation console several times. There was more going on than just a review from an ornery supervisor, though, and Charista knew it. She tapped controls with way more effort than necessary, and the display cycled through several very familiar views, but Charista knew the scrutiny was just part of the routine that was her life.

The navigation screen blinked, showing the plotted course of Omegan frigate *Trussel* in green, indicating a successful chart. Charista glanced up into Bezar's scowl and replied. "Course plot successful." *Do we have to go through this every single time?*

Bezar glanced past Charista at the display before he walked off with a series of grunts.

That's the nicest response I've gotten from most superior officers on this mission.

In reality, things could've been much worse for Charista, given her history and, more so, her family's history. Her father Findlay was executed for sharing troop moves with the enemy Railen. Findlay's action at the time was intended to be strategic, but it backfired in the worst way. After a challenging assignment in Omegan Retooling, where she reworked spent tech into being reusable, Charista was given her job on the *Trussel*.

Charista edged up from her seat and peeked up and down the hallway. She figured she at least had a few minutes, based on how often someone came by to second guess whatever she'd been doing. Her navigation duties handled for the moment, Charista took to her favorite hobby. In addition to course-plotting and comms, her console gave her access to Network.

Network's galaxy-wide collection of transmissions from comms, news reports, and recorded conversations was a mess. Without the benefit of good curation, the UA implemented the system in an attempt to spread information throughout Ling Galaxy. The growing efforts at maintaining distribution networks throughout Ling made it a challenge, so Network grew organically, about as orderly as the average mold spore colony.

The screech of static burst over the comm speakers until Charista adjusted the frequency enough. Still, the data stream, like a typical one from Network, was a long line of audio chatter and video clips. Finding helpful information on Network wasn't entirely impossible, but it was time-consuming without the benefit of a Sift Routine.

Once the Omegana Sift Routine appeared on Charista's screen, she disabled it. She entered her bypass codes she'd developed, which triggered a few warning messages. Omegana wasn't concerned about most of the information on Network, just the bits that dealt with troop moves and the UA. Charista wanted a deeper dive, so she'd created her own private Sift Routine. Charista flexed her fingers. Her father taught her ways around even the most stringent Omegan technological defenses, and those were thankfully still breakable with some effort. Omegana valued the power of a gun or blade far more than that of tech; a soft underbelly Charista was glad to exploit.

A clip about the Railen appeared and stopped Charista from her casual skim. The Railen race were already divided, but thanks to a well-organized Omegan assault, most of the Railen race were nomads. No word was given or even clear on where the Railen would end up, but a video of their motley collection of craft headed for an unknown destination looked sad to Charista.

Charista glanced into the hallway again. So far, she hadn't been spotted scanning Network with a non-Omegan Sift, which was forbidden since it was beyond her assigned duties.

Footsteps sounded down the corridor. Charista hid the Sift Scan and returned her console to the Navigation view. The footsteps got louder.

Charista craned her neck for a view and saw Isaac Pyatt nursing his handheld device as he walked. In the Omegana military, kiss-ups weren't discouraged, but bravery was what gave an Omegan soldier the awards and status they all craved. Isaac had mastered the kiss-up part for sure. However, he hadn't quite established himself in the bravery in battle category, which explained his assignment to *Trussel*. Isaac had only been out of the Omegan Academy a year before Charista, which was enough for him to outrank her.

She'd returned to her console, watching the indicator of the scan, a pulsating icon. She watched the screen for a few minutes until she heard Isaac immediately behind her.

"Status on our course?"

Charista stiffened and spun in her chair until she met Isaac's devious grin. "Calculated, with alternate intercepts factored in. I anticipated we'll run comms checks to planet Agmon before landing, so I brought our trajectory near the more populated side for an easier test."

Isaac nodded and tapped notes into his device, held close against his uniform's pressed gray fabric. *How can gray fabric have a shine?* The few ribbons on Isaac's chest area also seemed to glimmer mockingly. *Isaac must have little to do besides memorizing regulations into rote memory and how universally crucial those were to anything worthwhile. I bet his primary mission was finding the failings of those other than himself.* "Very good, I'll pass that along to the captain and -" His eyes focused past Charista toward the console.

Please let him not have seen anything. I hid the search, didn't I?

Isaac pointed toward Charista's screen. "What's that?"

Charista swallowed hard and turned slowly. *Of course - the Sift Routine had signaled completion; the flashing indicator on the screen was as subtle as a punch to the face.*

Charista's neck tightened as she scrambled for any halfway decent alibi. "Environmental analysis-"

"-Are you running a Sift?" asked Isaac.

Charista clenched her fists. Isaac had been a busybody to not just her but several others on the ship. Charista watched him previously breaking down crew over uniform code violations and even improper maintenance processes.

I bet the suck-up would make someone check the Trussel exterior mid-flight if he could've gotten away with it.

Once the initial wave of apprehension settled on Charista, it was replaced with one of her many mantras, calming focused thoughts she used in the months and years since her father's execution.

My path is forward, my cause is right, and no one will stop me.

Charista's mind, honed and developed through her early years of watching her father work, and her mother's warrior cunning intellect gave her faculties a sharp focus. But, that said, Charista also knew that while Isaac was an idiot, she had a role to play for the time, one of the dutiful officers who begged more than anything to remain in the good graces.

Once Charista relaxed, she replied to Isaac, who was still fixated on her screen. "You're pretty good at knowing regulations. Did you forget the one about scans of a planet without a confirmed Omegan presence before arrival? T85-13?"

Isaac's face simmered with resentment. Even a stickler like himself had to admit the rule of regulation was as gospel as any religion could've ever professed. Charista savored the change in his expression from triumphant whistleblower to off-put sycophant.

Isaac only replied, "Just report any required course deviations as soon as they are identified."

"Don't I always?"

Isaac's eyes narrowed. "Carry on." He thrust himself down the corridor.

Once Isaac turned the corner at the far end, Charista gave a shuddered sigh. It was a good play for her, and she wondered how many more she needed before getting to a position of power where she was the one to whom everyone else answered.

A series of aches bloomed along Charista's upper and lower back. The pains reminded her of how long she'd sat in her cubby. Her shift ran several hours, and the seat made that time feel way longer. She was in the middle of a half-hearted attempt at a stretch when several low-pitched creaks distracted Charista's attention. Two crew members dashed down the hallway past her cubby entrance a few moments later. She glanced out into the hall in their direction for a moment before she shook her head. The *Trussel* had such a reputation for malfunction it earned the far from desirable nickname, the "Trashel."

Charista caught a few words from the crew as they worked on the issue. Evidently, some stabilizers had malfunctioned and were being patched per the order of the day. *Trussel's* fate once they returned to Omegana wasn't filled with a lot of bright hope, but as long as they returned in one piece, that was enough for Charista.

The sound of boots clanking on metal drew Charista's attention up the hall. This time it was Kindra Montes. When their eyes met, Kindra smiled slightly as she walked up close.

"Are we done with this voyage yet?" Kindra asked.

Charista smiled a bit. Her tension eased at the sight of a friendly face for a change. Kindra came up with Charista in the Omegan academy, but the two knew each other from childhood. While news of Findlay's crime and sentencing drove most Omegans away from Charista, it hadn't lost her Kindra as a friend. Charista was grateful for Kindra's seeing through the perceived disloyalty of her father.

Charista sighed. "If only we were back at home port. But, I guess we have this mission to Agmon first, right?"

Kindra nodded. "Off to the lovely planet of Agmon, now that Malone Stanton has worked his magic on it. Of course, we don't get much play time, just a simple housing set up for an Omegan garrison."

"Yeah. Tell you something else; I'm done with Isaac Pyatt." Charista sighed.

Kindra shook her head violently at Charista's assessment. "It's bad enough being on this scrap heap of a frigate, but dealing with his issues too? What's his problem? Jerk gets good marks in training, so he sticks it to everyone else?"

"He got you too?" Charista asked.

"Yeah, on my analysis reports. We're supposed to run these scans of Agmon, right? Ensure we've got the best spots for the Omegan installation. He decides to review my report and contacts Captain Risberg about it. That little bastard got me my second reprimand inside of two weeks."

"Oh, that's right, your second... you little uniform code violator."

Charista shook her head as Kindra swiped at her arm. The only good thing about Kindra's news was it confirmed Isaac's diligent attention to all things procedural wasn't saved just for Charista. Instead, Isaac had the distinction of being an equal opportunity annoyer. "At least your father wasn't branded an enemy of the state. I'm lucky I wasn't permanently placed in a sanitation detail some-where." Charista's pained chuckle betrayed the truth behind her words.

Kindra patted her friend's arm. "It hasn't been easy for you, has it?"

Charista shook her head glumly.

"Guess I'll have to team up with Adarsha to cheer you up, as long as we can break her away from her post with Security." Adarsha, another classmate of Charista and Kindra's, shared space on the *Trussel* with them. The two were Charista's only saving grace on a ship where the rest of the crew saw Charista as some kind of infection to be cleared up as soon as possible.

Kindra glanced back up the hallway, then back to Charista. "Look at it this way. We're on this stretch for another four weeks, give or take. Once we're back on Omegana, we'll have a little break before our next deployment, especially if they get smart and finally ditch the *Trashel* - I mean, *Trussel.*"

That got a chuckle from Charista, and Kindra smiled at her friend's brief lift in spirit.

Charista stretched again, working on the endless knots in her back. "Guess I should get back to work. Wouldn't want to give Isaac another reason for a write-up."

"Right?" Kindra nodded. "OK. Let's meet in the galley next time our shifts line up."

Charista nodded with a smile, and Kindra took off down the hallway.

After a few more useless attempts at easing her back pains, Charista settled back into the hum drum of her work, eyeing the onboard systems of *Trussel* and checking the ship's progress on its designated course. Her almost serene focus was jolted when the comm squawked to life with several voices. The Omegan Horde, deployed sections of the Omegan army, proceeded throughout Ling Galaxy on various missions. The underlying directive ordered there were never less than two Horde units in proximity of each other, ready to consolidate if any team needed extra firepower, while keeping their overall objective of canvassing as much of Ling Galaxy as possible.

The view on Charista's console, showing a holographic chart of Ling Galaxy, flickered several times. Charista tapped the display panel, correcting the issue. The stars and systems of Ling floated about the room. A blue line indicated the *Trussel's* position and course all the way to its end destination. Charista switched her view to the rest of the nearby planets. Together with Malone Stanton, the Omegan goal was to canvas Ling Galaxy and lay claim to it, one piece at a time. Yassel was the ultimate prize, but the more footholds they established first, the more the UA control of Ling slipped away.

Since Isaac made his regular round by Charista, she figured she at least had a little time to contact Joanna. Charista knew she still had to be careful - communicating with the Railen, sworn enemies of the Omegans, was a fast track to imprisonment at the very least. Despite the risk, Charista craved the moments with Joanna. It was her last link to her father's memory, someone who knew him as Joanna did.

Charista hoped she timed her next round of supervisor checks as she closed the portal to her cubby and activated the comm to Joanna. Charista immediately noticed Joanna's former Railen uniform, or what was left of it. The garb Joanna still wore from her Railen outfit was reduced to a single patch, but she kept it along with a heavy cloak, with her uniform remnants as a sash around her neck.

"You're hell-bent on keeping that, aren't you?" Charista asked.

Joanna's eyes closed with a knowing grin. "I'm a Railen, Charista. Vengeance is in our DNA."

"Not unlike Omegans," Charista replied. They shared a laugh over their respective heritage of betrayal and abandonment. Joanna's contributions helped her fellow Railen from their start as bastard Nara outcasts to a technologically capable race. She gave them the tools that went with the raging lust for power and revenge that was homegrown.

"How are you doing since the flight?"

Joanna shrugged. "It was hard and still is. We've settled on a moon around planet Cerulia. We had a few vehicles tucked away, so we'll be regrouping in little time."

"I guess we'll run into each other out here at some point," Charista's throat tightened in worry about the idea of her and Joanna on two opposite sides in the same conflict. The average Omegan had no use for the Railen and weren't at all beyond obliterating the Railen, and the feeling was mutual. The attack of the Omegans on the former Railen stronghold at Delfina was just another in a series of pushes each side made against the other.

The warmth in Joanna's face faded. "Listen, dear. I know you've got plenty to worry about already, but I have to tell you something."

Charista leaned in closer to the screen. The fragile system she'd set up with Joanna depended on many things, and a possible change in any of that worried her.

"The Brescar shipments were halted." While Essence remained the primary source of life and energy in Ling Galaxy, many attempted to replicate a usable substitute. Brescar was Findlay's attempt, and while well worth the effort, the volatility associated with the substance was too much for Omegana to use. The excess quantities of Brescar were kept with the plans by Omegana of disposing the stuff one day, once the Omegan conquest was less of a priority. Findlay, and Charista after his death, arranged for Brescar to be sent secretly to Joanna, who carried on the work to make Brescar a viable energy source in Ling Galaxy one day.

"Halted?" Charista said the word with a mix of surprise and annoyance.

Joanna nodded.

"I'll check with Edin when I get back to Omegana. That's all I can do." Charista took a shuddered breath as she felt her pulse rattle in her throat. "Will this ever get easier?" She knew Joanna had no answer for that, but still asking the question made her feel like she was doing...something.

Charista rubbed the back of her aching neck. She was in a race for several things but only felt like she slipped further behind with each day. *Things have to work out at some point. Joanna's smart like Dad; she'll get Brescar usable somehow. Besides ruling Omegana, energy dominance is the only other true power in Ling Galaxy.*

Joanna gave a pained smile in response. "It's OK, dear. We've just got to keep pushing."

The determination in Joanna's voice made Charista realize since the Railen kept up their crusade after all the horrible situations they faced, there was no reason Charista couldn't have persevered either.

"I'm closing this comm for now, so I don't test my luck any further," Charista smiled and added a wave.

Joanna grinned in kind as their transmission ended.

Charista returned to glances at Network and the other part of her job, checking the comm transmissions for anything that affected the *Trussel's* mission. While most of the comm was standard Horde transmissions, giving unit numbers, locations, and status, one message broke over the rest and caught Charista's attention, just by the name it mentioned.

"Stanton has been sighted near far reach planet Tausian. Requesting assistance."

Oh, the god needs help from Mother Omegana now?

Charista scoffed. The Omegans had entered into a pact with Malone Stanton, thanks to their Emperor Zakmar. Zakmar was most interested in Omegan domination of Ling Galaxy, but was shrewd enough not to butt heads with Malone, at least for a time. Instead, Zakmar saw in Malone a chance for them to side with a huge threat and take Malone's attention off Omegana, so Zakmar could one day have a structure in place to handle Malone and keep him in control.

A quick scan of the sector of Ling for Tausian showed a few Horde units in proximity, so Charista repointed the message to those groups, notifying them of the issue.

Malone has everyone eating out of his hand. He'll be at my feet one day, just like everyone else.

An alert klaxon blared on the comm and activated the video

screen on the unit. Charista was startled by the image of Commander Chun on screen. After a moment, she snapped a salute.

"Connect me to Risberg immediately."

"T-the captain, sir?" Charista asked.

Chun's brow creased. "Are you deaf, ensign? Transfer, now!"

Charista forwarded the communication to Captain Risberg. She wondered what was so urgent about their mission. The *Trussel's* trek was light years from conquest for the action hungry who wanted only a long and violent spar with the enemy. The *Trussel's* primary foe was boredom. Her threat, sagging crew morale over being relegated to one of the more meaningless assignments in the eyes of Omegans like the Horde.

A series of chimes echoed through the halls, indicating the current shift's end. Charista leaned back in her seat in relief. *It seemed like it would never get here.* As she collected her things, she thought about all the pieces in play... Malone, Joanna, the Railen, the Omegans, even pitiful little Isaac. *So many options, just what to do with them all?*

It was a question for another time.

Once the *Trussel* reached a distance of three standard days from Agmon, Captain Risberg called a crew briefing to review deployment procedures and confirm all crew assignments.

Charista was headed to the meeting when a hand grabbed her arm and stopped her short, and her eyes met those of Commander Pit Darin, or simply "Pit." Pit was larger than the average Omegan, with a resting scowl and broad frame that gave most Omegans second thoughts about grappling with him. He began his Omegana military career during the last few years of Nara Service. The scars that adorned his face and arms hinted at plenty of stories, and Charista knew she wasn't interested in hearing any of them.

"Where you going, traitor?"

Charista's face flushed hot. "Heading to the briefing as ordered, sir."

Pit gnashed his jaw. His face had the usual greenish scales of the average Omegan, with an extra assortment of scars. Charista forced back a gag reflex at the odor of Pit's breath, which reeked with a rancid rotted meat smell and some strange hint of something burnt. For any junior officer, joining a new crew came with at least a few moments of harassment by one or more senior Omegan officers, and Pit had bucked for the position of high priest of the Omegan Church of War for a long time.

"Just because you're on this ship don't mean I got to like it. You're on my watch, so keep your mouth shut and follow orders. I'll jettison you outta here if you get on my bad side, understand?"

"Affirmative." Charista's voice was low, her eyes locked into Pit's. After a moment, Pit grunted and sauntered off.

The briefing was short and sweet. Omegans were coming to establish their own Garrison on Agmon to extend the reach of the Horde, and *Trussel* was delivering supplies needed for their forward base. The crew was instructed to keep scans out for the UA craft since the movement of supplies to Agmon was sure to arouse UA attention. While *Trussel* had armaments, it was short on the kind of weaponry for a full-out battle if the UA moved to overpower and confiscate their craft for any number of trumped-up UA violations.

Pit Darin assigned the crew tasks on Agmon to deploy the Omegan base structure. While Kindra and Adarsha were given set up and configuration tasks, Charista's assignment kept her onboard, running the analysis for the return trip. She'd have liked a slight bit of on-planet time. Long voyages locked on starcraft weren't great for the psyche, but Charista figured with Pit in charge of her welfare, she wasn't getting comfort anytime soon. *I'm sure Isaac has his little hand-picked list of ground crew, and I'm a few light years away from being included there.*

* * *

Once the troops aboard *Trussel* and those already on site organized their operations, *Trussel* left Agmon, returning to Omegana. As productive as the primary mission had been, Charista's ultimate goal needed more simmering before it was ready. Her biggest fear at that point was not knowing what happened to Edin and the Brescar deliveries. *Either he was killed or arrested.* Neither was good, but an arrest would've brought more trouble than her reputation already invited.

Chapter Two

O N HER NEXT SHIFT DURING the voyage home, Charista returned to her Network Sift when a wave of emotion hit her and instantly stopped her thoughts. It happened like that, from time to time. She'd been fine, focused on her work, plans, and sadness struck her without warning. She knew what it was when it happened, though. She was an adult orphan, trying to figure things out. There wasn't even the shell of Omegana's camaraderie to comfort her. While the average Omegan had plenty of news and stories about the Horde wreaking havoc in Ling to stir their pride and bolster their spirits, the nation and its goals diverted from Charista's awhile back. She was along for the ride but wasn't in for any benefits.

Charista's latest Network Sift run brought back more information, but she wasn't sure how much was helpful. She flipped through reports from the UA on just how well they thought Ling Galaxy held on during the tough times, chatter from the Railen, dealing with their recent exile, and various fragments of transmissions from Syndicates around Ling Galaxy: soldiers for hire and those who managed a profit even when so many faced starvation.

Your parents are gone.

Charista blinked the tears away and waited for the feeling to pass. It did; it just sometimes took a bit. But she was ready; she'd wait until she felt better. This time it held a bit more, so she shut her eyes and reached for the controls on her screen. She'd done the task enough, first in training in the Academy and then later in prep for her assignment. The job wasn't overly complex and easy enough that the routine diverted attention from the pain she felt. It would get easier one day, she promised herself. She just didn't know when.

After so many hours of searching through the endless geyser of information, the data and video streams became a blur to her. She'd looked away for a moment, feeling another bout coming over her emotions, when she glanced back and saw something unexpected on the screen.

This could be something... a report on a movement of Xeno from planet Zormad to Yassel and UA headquarters. The UA is engaging with the Omegans and others all over Ling; why risk sending a transport through all the fray? That's pretty boneheaded, even for the UA. Still, Charista's curiosity was yanked quite firmly toward the story, so she dug further.

The reports were few, but it was unusual enough that she found them fascinating. The Xeno had made an unremarkable entrance into Ling as a fledgling race on a feeble ark ship. No one knew what brought Xeno to Ling Galaxy, but they seemed mostly harmless from all appearances.

The Xeno were an interesting case to those who took a little time and studied their story a little deeper. The debate in Ling Galaxy over many things washed over the Xeno, while some barely considered them a footnote. It wasn't until rumors spread about the Nara taking an interest in the Xeno that Charista thought there might be some value in the derelict race. After all, they'd not only been enduring the rough, unfamiliar conditions of Ling Galaxy itself, but the Xeno had made a dangerous, even crazy trek over numerous sectors from a distant galaxy to Ling. As powerless as they may have been, they showed they had more than enough stamina for who knew what else.

Charista adjusted the scan from *Trussel's* course toward the UA transport ship headed to Yassel and thoroughly checked the contents. Detailed charts appeared, listing counts of lifeforms aboard, ages, and other vital information. She stored the output of the personnel tallies on a Data Tag and stuffed it in one of the inner folds of her uniform.

In any case, Charista believed the Xeno weren't as mewling as what most of Ling had written them off as. The Railen had a few runs with the Xeno, but it was a mess for the Railen, at least at first. The Xeno fought back and killed several Railen in the process, and when the Railen returned to finish the job on the Xeno, even that mission wasn't a complete success.

The Xeno are as much a bastard race as the Railen, but they're tough. Maybe they'd be interested in some kind of alliance. They probably just want to survive. They could be handy if the rumors I've heard about them and Essence are true.

She gathered her notes and headed for the captain's quarters. Kai Risberg, captain of the *Trussel*, had seen his share of fights in his youth, a time that had passed him by a bit. But, in his middle-aged Omegan years, he managed a commanding authority over the crew of the *Trussel* and ran the ship without insubordination.

Charista snapped a salute at the entrance to Risberg's quarters. "Sir, thank you for agreeing to see me. I wanted you to know soon as I found out." Charista activated her display tablet and held it out for Risberg. He eyed the device for a moment as if it was a questionable piece of meat. "What exactly am I looking at?"

"Sir, it's the Xeno. I know they're not a serious threat to our mission, but I think we're overlooking something valuable there. The UA has just sent a mission through the lines to planet Zormad to bring the Xeno to Yassel."

Risberg steepled his fingers and leaned back in thought. For a moment, Charista beamed in anticipation of his praise for her insight. Just because the *Trussel* was on the low order of service in the

Omegan fleet, it hadn't meant the ship or its crew had nothing valuable to offer.

However, with an annoyed grunt, Risberg arched his brow and stared blankly at Charista. "So what?"

"Sir, we have enough Horde deployed throughout Ling. The UA convoy is fairly light. It wouldn't take much Omegan craft to overtake it and grab that asset. If the Xeno are that important to the UA, that makes them important to us, so we should intercept that convoy. Anything that hurts the UA has to be good for us, right?"

Risberg leaned back in his seat as his eyes narrowed. Charista had been in the captain's service long enough to know what came next wasn't anything on the order of a glorious citation of her enterprising discovery. "Ensign Mantisword..." Risberg said Charista's rank with the emphasis like her even having that rank was a slam against the Omegan military. "You've been assigned to this ship because you've distinguished yourself in the last piss hole they stuck you in. Don't for a moment think I forgot what put you there. I lost good troops in that maneuver your father leaked to the Railen. I don't want to hear any more about your searches in Ling Galaxy, which are unauthorized and unnecessary. Omegana has her sights on all of Ling Galaxy. This takes a wide-reaching effort by the Horde, Ensign. You'll learn what that means one day. The Omegans won't be avoided; we'll be around. If this convoy is en route to Yassel as you say it is, they'll be found, either en route or when we advance on UA headquarters in time. That's enough for now. Get back to your post, and don't bother me again unless it's related to your duties."

Captain Risberg pointed to the door before he returned to his viewscreen, a readout of the *Trussel's* current course and nearby planets of note on it. Charista snapped a salute so sharply that the fabric on her uniform gave a loud rustle. "Aye aye, sir." Charista spun on one heel and left.

Charista felt her face flush hot as she walked back to her post. *Why do they even bother giving me any assignment besides rooting through the junk in Retooling? They'll never listen to my ideas until they get something useful handed to them.*

Back in her station, she activated a scan for the portion of Ling Galaxy where the UA transport had likely been and ran a search for Omegan craft in the vicinity. She smiled when the battle cruiser *Praximus* came into view. *I don't care what Risberg thinks. We can't let this pass by. Intercepting an innocent convoy would be easy for the Praximus, the way Captain Ve Bartosik thought of himself as the Prince Hunter of Omegana.*

Charista smiled as she again disabled the normal processes on her panel. Her father's skills worked through her again, and she found herself able to create a very official-looking transmission.

"Attention *Praximus*: large convoy leaving planet Zormad en route to Yassel. Passengers and cargo aboard are believed to be Xeno, among other valuables for the UA. Proceed at once on an intercept course. Slaughter all that are not of Xeno origin and return craft and contents to Omegana."

Charista smirked at the message. She knew the lies in the text were more than necessary to give her people and herself a chance at finding the true path to power in their fight.

Her insides knotted up with tension at realizing what she'd just done. Spoofing a comm wasn't the best idea for anyone who wanted to keep a low profile, but the chance at grabbing the Xeno seemed worth the risk. *Malone has his spectacles; the Horde have their conquests. Omegans respond best to bargaining chips. It's about time I collect some. I just know there's something to these Xeno, and if I can help them, maybe they can return the favor.*

Chapter Three

FINALLY, CHARISTA'S SHIFTS WITH Kindra and Adarsha lined up, and they met in the *Trussel's* Galley. The large room hosted seating for a hundred, roughly one-fourth of the crew onboard the freighter. A serving area at one end offered the best barely digestible rations the Omegan military was forced to provide. After getting their servings of glorified animal feed, Charista and her friends grabbed a table at the far end of the hallway from the entrance. Charista worked on eating while Adarsha and Kindra filled her in on their work on Agmon. They talked over the general crowd noise as others on the same shift grabbed their food and chatted with their table mates.

"Charista, you would've hated Agmon. I mean, the temperate climate, the fresh air," Adarsha rolled her eyes.

Charista threw a balled-up napkin at her friend's face. She relished the times they had like this, sporadic as they were.

"Serious, what was it like down there? I saw lush trees on the video screens." Charista eyed her friends like a lawyer waiting for a witness' response.

Kindra glanced at Adarsha, who had a mouthful of food, then

back to Charista. "It's something. I'm amazed by what Malone did there. The preliminary scan data we had on that place showed it near extinction. Even with the modest supply of Essence the planet had, it wouldn't be long for it."

"Then, how did Malone adding more of the same Essence make it suddenly so better?"

Adarsha swallowed her bite of food. She glanced at Kindra before she replied, "I dunno about that, but I know this one won't admit she's in love with Malone and already believes he can do anything. Me, I can't figure it out either."

"Shut up," Kindra elbowed Adarsha in her midsection. Adarsha recoiled back with a series of giggles.

"At least Malone is better than those filthy Railen," Adarsha added.

Kindra's face bunched up in disgust. "Please, we're trying to eat here. Don't ever bring up those scum around me. The best day for Ling is when all Railen are dead."

Charista met Kindra's eyes and saw the search for approval in her friend's glance. Charista swallowed the lump that formed at the thought of Joanna and gave a quick nod in reply. *There's no way they can know about Joanna and me. But what about what I did with the Praximus comm? Would they have thought it was a good idea?*

A warm surge shot through Charista's frame, and she glanced downward in silence regarding her food. Soon, she felt a touch on her arm and looked into Adarsha's eyes.

"What's wrong?"

Oh, I'd love to tell you. I wish I could. But that would only involve you, and I can't do that to you, my friend.

"Oh, Pit was giving me trouble before the pre-Agmon briefing."

"That old slug?" Kindra shook her head. "I've had enough of him too. He's still riding that rep from years ago when he was a chief of a Nara unit. Times have changed. He's not so tough jockeying the 'Trashel' now. Some Omegans have to tell themselves they're not the decrepit burnouts they are."

Adarsha smiled and nodded in reply. "Don't let Pit bother you, Charista."

Charista nodded. *It wasn't much of a lie, and it was as much of the truth I wanted to share. Oh, my friends... what is going to happen to us? How can I do what I need to overtake Omegana and not hurt you?*

Adarsha smiled warmly, her eyes filled with concern for her friend. "Look, let's just finish this voyage. I'll grab you for some sparring when we get home before our next posting. Get your mind off things for a while."

Charista nodded. With a shaky breath, she patted Adarsha's hand on the table. "Deal."

The threesome finished their so-called meal and headed for the exit, with Charista trailing slightly behind. Seeing her friends in person, like in old times, gave her a feeling of peace. Unfortunately, the momentary serenity was shattered by a hand firmly gripping her shoulder. She stopped short and looked over into the smug gaze of Isaac Pyatt.

"Captain Risberg wants to see you. He found out about your stunt with the *Praximus* and is pretty upset."

"Of course he is."

* * *

Charista mulled her possible responses on her walk to the Captain's quarters. *We're at war. Why wouldn't we share strategic information with fellow troops?* But Risberg, like the *Trussel*, had accepted their state in the universe as couriers, not combatants. She wondered what he did to earn the military honors on his uniform.

Risberg's expression was way different from Charista's last visit with him. Instead of the disconnected glance of someone preoccupied, he now peered at Charista with eyes that blazed like angry coals on a fire.

Charista took the hot seat with no fanfare. She clutched the arms of the chair and braced for impact. Risberg said nothing for a while.

Then, after a lengthy glare directly into Charista's eyes, he prodded about, the only other sound in the room, a series of disgruntled groans. Opening arguments by the good captain were wordless, but Charista had a fair enough idea of what her sentence would be.

"Ensign Mantisword, you and I have a problem."

Charista squeezed the arms of her seat so tightly that her hands felt like they were on fire. It hadn't stopped her racing mind, and it sure hadn't eased the heavy soreness in her midsection as she eyed Captain Risberg like a condemned prisoner awaiting execution of sentence. *Risberg believes a Captain is god of their ship, and all heretics of that religion are subject to the full wrath.* She had no idea what that involved, which only worsened her panic. Risberg was undoubtedly from the old order of Omegans, who according to stories, trained their ranks in torture camps intending to make the soldiers as resistant to pain as possible. The scars on Risberg's arms and face provided evidence that those stories were more than Omegan legend.

In an instant, Risberg clutched Charista's arms and leaned into her, his face mere inches from hers. The stale stench of his breath triggered Charista's gag reflex.

I thought the food in the Trussel galley smelled terrible.

Charista gasped and felt cold sweat bathe her entire body. She saw his gaze, even though she avoided eye contact.

"You see," Risberg began, "I worked with your father in the Science Wing. A seasoned warrior now and then gets called in for testing equipment Findlay and his team built. While all Omegans were expected to be battle ready, we accepted those with the most capable minds served Omegana better in labs than on the battlefield. So, I knew Findlay. I can't say his betrayal surprised me. On the contrary, it was almost a relief to me when I heard about it. I hated that someone with as low tolerance and resolve as Findlay Mantisword had gotten away with the accolades he did. And then, you, his daughter, were assigned to my ship. I couldn't have cared less what kind of military mind your mother was - I fought against having your traitor blood under my command at first. But then, I wondered, what if I lost you in an accident? A frigate isn't known for combat engagements, but after all, with the war we're in, who's to say we weren't overrun? I can't imagine many on this ship would've questioned something like that. But, still, my code to protect my crew held fast."

Charista swallowed a large lump in her throat. She lost the ability to speak but felt it wasn't the right time anyway.

Sure enough, Risberg continued, first grabbing Charista's chin and guiding her head until she looked deep into Risberg's eyes.

"The only reason you're not being vaporized is that the Horde confirmed the info and are on an intercept now. But, that doesn't excuse your flagrant disregard for my order. You're on very shaky ground with me, young Ensign. I'll be getting reports from you daily via Isaac. And, you better believe you and your activities will be monitored for the rest of this voyage."

"Sir, I had what I thought was good intelligence -"

"-on a cargo of puny Xeno. You ignored my direct orders and sent the notice out to Captain Ve. I'm not interested in the result. Your insubordination is unacceptable. A chain of command is first a chain. And, you broke it. If you can't follow small orders, you can't be trusted to follow large ones."

Risberg slammed his desk as punctuation to his sentence. His gaze bored deep into Charista's eyes. Her pulse rattled in her throat, and she felt a wave of heat as it flashed over her entire face.

Risberg leaned in close once again. "You're confined to research duties for the rest of this mission. You'll review fleet schematics for the rest of this voyage. That should give you time to think about the value of following orders from your commanding officer."

With a single gesture, Risberg dismissed Charista from his quarters. There was no point in any objections, and she knew it. Risberg was judge and jury on his ship, and she had no plans on testing the executioner part. Her trip back was more painful this time around. Charista's gloom lifted a little when she saw Adarsha coming toward her in the hallway.

"We saw Isaac grab you in the galley. What happened?" Adarsha's eyes were full of concern for her friend.

Charista slumped against the nearby wall. "I'm restricted to research for the rest of this trip."

"Why?"

Charista leaned against the bulkhead until it felt like it would either break off into space or absorb her into it. "I sent a comm to the *Praxiumus* against Captain's orders."

"Why?"

Charista looked up slowly at her friend. "I saw intel that the UA sent a convoy to transport Xeno back to Yassel. Risberg said to ignore it, but I alerted them anyway."

Adarsha's face twisted in pain. "That was a bad idea. He's no hero of mine, either, but he's still the Captain."

"I know, I know." Charista folded her arms and glanced up the hallway.

"Was this what was bugging you at lunch?"

Well, that and the fact I'm working with Joanna, a Railen you and pretty much every other Omegan wants to kill. "Yeah, you could say that."

"Well, it's done. If you want my advice, let things fall where they do on the Xeno. You're better not to get involved with them."

Charista met Adarsha's eyes again. "Won't be too hard for the rest of this mission; no more comm or nav for me. I guess my meals will be handed through the door."

A tear formed in Adarsha's eye. "At least you're not in the brig."

"This will make my review back at home even more interesting." Charista sighed.

"That's still going on?"

"Of course. My dad was an enemy of the state, remember? They watch me hard even when I follow the rules."

The two friends hugged while Charista cried a bit into Adarsha's shoulder. Unfortunately, Charista was again relegated to being ignored, reminded how she was a blight on Omegana that needed to be kept in a vacuum in the hope she one day withered and died. Once they released their embrace, Charista took a few steps down the hall before she looked back at Adarsha through tear-soaked eyes. Adarsha held her hand to her chest, her voice a pained whisper.

"Hang in there!"

* * *

The *Trussel* ship library was musty, which was quite the accomplishment for a facility that hosted a collection of digital books. The shabby room owed its rank smell to virtual non-use. The Science Wing had provided the materials in the room, but beyond that, the library served very little use to most of her crew. While ships like *Trussel* were equipped with documentation on the Omegan fleet, the average Omegan's interest in the literary, even informational prose, wasn't even slight. Weapons and fisticuffs were way higher on the list of leisure time activities than reading.

A lone robotic camera watched the table in the center of the room, which was Charista's new workstation for the rest of her trip. The smooth gray and black steel arc fixture that ended in a very ominous-looking eye lens reminded Charista that as much as she thought and felt that she was utterly alone in the room, she never was. She wondered what they'd have expected her to do in a sealed room with no access to comms other than the ship address system.

Wow, these chairs suck. Charista nestled as best she could against the firm unforgiving steel seat and chairback and pulled up schematics. Her eyes began to swim after the first few hours, and her mind drifted in and out of clearness.

Charista did that, of course, until her mind kicked back into gear. In the idleness Risberg sentenced her to, Charista's mind took more than enough opportunity to reassess her situation. While Charista visually digested diagrams, specification charts, and designs of the Omegan starcraft in use along with the experimental variants, she forced thoughts of her situation into her mind to keep herself feeling productive.

This is just a setback. Risberg will try to fry me on my review for this. I've just got to take this all one move at a time. I'll get through this review, and Joanna will get Brescar working right. We just have to get to that next step.

Chapter Four

THE ENGINES OF *TRUSSEL* SLOWED to a deep rumble as the craft eased its way to the port on Omegana. The vessel made contact with the landing platform with a mild jolt. Charista smirked at the other crew who'd stumbled at the sudden halt of their ship.

A series of air jets blasted outside, and the central gangway lowered slowly. Charista followed the rest onto the dock boarding area and into the processing facility. As a Frigate crew, they didn't have nearly the armaments or gear to deal with as the infantry units carried, so their trip through the facility wasn't long. Several bins were about, and Omegan supply personnel stood nearby to receive any spent med packs, charge units, and various odds and ends from their run in space.

The crew of *Trussel* arrived back on Omegana without much fanfare. The ongoing war required regular attention by Zakmar and members of the Omegan military machine, so the customaries like greeting a returning crew were gone. For the rest of Charista's shipmates, their return meant time back at home port: visiting with families and a few typical days of R&R. For Charista, it meant days of solitude. Only this time, something else went with it: her usual review board, but with the extra job of determining what her actions on *Trussel* deserved in the way of punishment.

Once their crew was dismissed, Charista wandered about the port and surrounding areas. Her pack strewn over her back, she walked a bit through the streets of her city.

The city of Gajanan, the capital of Omegana, was always busy with activity. Transport crafts carried companies of Horde troops on deployments. The large, bullet-shaped starcraft lurched gracefully into the air until they reached orbital status. Smaller craft darted about the area in lower overhead patterns, carrying passengers and supplies around. Zakmar's push for Omegans to dominate Ling Galaxy sure hadn't hurt business.

The vast hulking structures of the Omegan Military and Science wings greeted Charista silently on her walk. She pulled the straps on her bag tighter and breathed in the fresh air for the first time in a while. She was cooped up for so long, and the soreness in her lower back and legs had left them with an annoying throb, so she figured it best if she walked a bit before she returned to her housing unit.

She hoped she found out whatever happened with the Brescar shipments quickly. One Omegan would've had an explanation, provided they were still around to give it. Still, with Risberg's eyes on her, she worried about contacts out in the open. So, for the time, she settled for a stroll to work out the body cramps her confined voyage left her.

The air in Gajanan was hot. The pungent smell of spent munitions tickled Charista's nose. The latest crop of military trainees was at it, of course. She glanced toward the Omegan training facility and saw a collection of Omegan starcraft on their tarmac, surrounded by a group of recruits. Not long ago, Charista was one of them. She paused for a moment and watched the eager Omegan military hopefuls, reminiscing on how her life was so much easier not that long ago.

Omegan residences in Gajanan city were somewhat nicer than in less municipal areas. Towering structures, with designs that weren't too different than the facilities for the Omegan Military Instruction and government building. Black, smooth steel columns jut from the surface upward into collections of windowed habitats, arranged in a honeycomb fashion.

Charista still had time before Risberg could've tried anything. The Review Board took a few days to assemble, given the state of Omegana's multiple troop deployments around Ling Galaxy. Zakmar's quest bled the homeland of some of its law and order, a necessary cost for the ultimate goal of conquest.

A sudden touch on Charista's arm stopped her short. Her guts tensed up, and she slowly looked back to see Adarsha's smiling face.

"Hey! I'm going to see my folks. How about we meet tomorrow?"

Charista nodded. "Well, I don't know when they'll call me in, so if it happens, I'll let you know."

Adarsha smiled and grabbed Charista's shoulder. The two shared a look that said enough. Charista grinned at her friend as they parted.

Charista swung past one of the Omegan Supply depots next. Several Omegans walked past her on her wandering trip home. She passed a group of Omegans that wore the tell-tale patch of the prison facility. She wondered just what it was like in the Omegan penal complex. Her father's crimes were too severe for him to be there very long, and since she'd already done a stint on the Retooling service, she wasn't eager to give her superiors any ideas about shoving her in that direction. The Review she faced could've handled that anyway. She figured she'd have let that come in time if that's what it was to be.

She began to think about the evening's meal when she heard a sharp whisper to her right.

"Hey!"

The voice came from a close by a group of power replicators. The structures were scattered about Omegana. They powered the energy grid of planet Omegana. Their trademark deep hum was so familiar that the average Omegan dismissed the white noise, which allowed her to hear the whisper that was barely louder than the equipment.

Charista stepped closer and noticed the tip of a boot from around the far corner. "Edin, is that you?"

Edin Herlan had known Charista since childhood when they played games before the worries of life became too big to ignore. He hadn't the physical stamina that a dedicated Horde trooper required, and his intellect wasn't the sharpest. Still, he made up for it with a very diligent work ethic, which gave him more than enough assignments in the Omegan machine, seeing to the fitting of Omegan starcraft, moving cargoes about, and whatever else needed doing at the time. However, Findlay had taken notice of Edin's drive and had him do basic delivery work for the Science Wing.

Edin poked his head around with a slight smile. "Sorry, I wanted to talk with you."

"It's OK. I know why."

In addition to Edin's reputation in the Omegan supply chain, he helped Charista set up a delivery method for Brescar to Joanna.

Charista stepped behind the power replicator, away from the walking path and hopefully out of earshot of the passerby Omegans.

"Joanna said there was a break in her Brescar supply."

Edin shook his head. "I did everything I could, but with Zakmar stepping up operations, the demand for supplies from Military and the Supply Depot shot up too. They've pulled our standard deliveries and redirected them to the Horde."

"They must've seen you loading Brescar if they caught you by surprise."

Edin glanced downward. "Yeah, they did. I told them I was working on disposal."

Good thinking, Edin. They already think the stuff is too volatile to be around. "Was that good enough for them?"

Edin shrugged. "For now. They're more concerned with keeping the Horde stocked up." Edin's eyes were full of worry. "What will we do about the rest of the Brescar and Joanna?"

Charista smiled and clasped Edin's hand. "Don't worry. Just keep in touch. I'm going back home, and I'll think of something." She heard herself say the words and knew she honestly had no idea what she was going to do. Nevertheless, it still felt better saying she'd come up with something. She only hoped that eventually became the truth.

Edin gave an understanding nod. "I'll be waiting. You know where to find me."

Charista kissed Edin lightly on the lips, and they parted. Like anything in her plans, the contact with Edin was a risk but a calculated one.

* * *

Charista arrived back at her housing unit 813. It hadn't been the same since Findlay's death, and it never would be again. She flung her pack on the dining table and lept into a chair, pausing for a long stretch. The material wasn't the most plush, but it was eons better than that chair on the *Trussel*. Her uniform was dirty and needed cleaning before the Inquiry.

Laundry can wait. She sighed in the silence of the room as her worries for the moment gradually drifted away from her.

After a while, she pulled up to a seated position. Her extended walk home helped her soreness out to a point, but there were still more pains to address. With a series of stretches, she worked her muscles that went sore with the idle sitting, especially in the library. She got to her feet and strode from the front room to the study area, where a large monitor on the wall greeted her. The display rotated between Omegana updates and Network in general.

Her home comm rang; it was Kindra.

"Well, hey there," Charista beamed.

Kindra smiled in kind. "I hope you're doing OK; they didn't waste time on new assignments for me. I've been redirected to a unit supporting one of Malone's new projects."

Malone was so active; he's even affecting my few close friends. "Wow, so when are you shipping out?"

"Couple of days. Have they set your review date yet?"

"No, maybe they need time to muster, with so many leaders out in forward Horde operations," Charista added a heavy sigh to her statement.

"I was hoping we three could have another day to relax together. If you can get Adarsha, you two should do something. I'll be thinking about you, my friend!"

Charista touched the screen, wishing the contact could've been directly on Kindra's face. "Me too. You be good, and we'll see each other soon."

Charista ended the comm and let her thoughts drift back to the Xeno. Stories about them had spread around Ling Galaxy like a virus. Some believed they had the potential to not only locate Essence but manipulate it. But the unknown was always an excellent place for rumors and speculation.

She thought about people who may have had an idea of the Xeno's worth. She wished she'd have been with the Science Wing on Omegana for a change. They had the first crack at the Xeno and what potential they had. But she'd been forbidden, and her father Findlay's record ensured that Charista and the Mantiswords were never allowed in again.

But she remembered someone who could've had an idea about the Xeno. She sure knew enough about the Omegans already.

Charista pulled her modified comm from its hiding place. She'd learned more than a little from her father over the years and had developed a comm untraceable by Omegans for contacting Joanna.

Joanna smiled at Charista's face when their session began.

"Hello dear, I still can't get over you as an officer now." Joanna beamed.

Charista shrugged. She appreciated the attention Joanna gave her and the interest she took. The void Charista felt over having no family on Omegana for sharing good news was slightly lessened by Joanna and her kindness. "They've done everything they can to keep me at the lowest level of responsibility. And my latest bout may keep me there for good."

"What happened?"

"Oh, I spotted a UA transport and asked my commander about it. I thought it was strange, the UA doing that through a war zone. But Captain Risberg hadn't any thought about following it. Instead, he thought it was a waste of time and ordered me to focus on my duties. But still, I sent the info to an Omegan cruiser, and it led to the capture of the Xeno."

Joanna nodded. "Strange thing to get punished for."

"Well, Captain Risberg specifically ordered me not to."

"And you did it anyway." Joanna's eyes drifted downward.

"It was risky, careless, even stupid given my family history... I know that. It could've been a cargo of food or something minor. It wouldn't have been the first time Network was wrong."

"Are you OK?" Joanna asked.

"My review board will rehash what I did and find new ways to make me miserable. Other than that, I'm just lovely."

Joanna nodded. "That was a bad idea, Charista. Still, it sounds like it paid off, more than they'd let you know, I bet. As for the Xeno, they've got some strange properties. I've studied them a bit, and we've sure had a rough time with them. I think they may be useful with Essence, maybe even Brescar too."

"Why can't Brescar just replace Essence? Wasn't that the whole idea?"

Joanna nodded. "Of course it was. However, Brescar still has a lot of volatility. I'm working on that, and your supply helps my experiments and modifications."

"About that supply," Charista said, "I have to figure out a new delivery chain for you. Edin was caught up in the expanded deliveries to Horde units, and we don't have access to the craft like before."

Joanna's lips formed a line. "I understand. I hope I can get replication working at some point, so I can duplicate the Brescar you've already sent. Until that happens, I'll be praying you restore delivery somehow."

Charista said, "I'll let you know. Alright, enough about me, how are things with you? What have you been cooking up over there?"

"Well, I've been working with the Brescar and got some of it weaponized."

Charista was stunned. She'd heard Findlay talk about energy properties of Brescar, and at the very most outside of that, a chance it gave a tremendous amount of speed to ships, maybe even rivaling the Transient Warp drives that remained fastest in Ling Galaxy for the moment. "How does that even work with the instability issues?"

Joanna smirked. "I've been tuning Brescar over time. It's been slow but promising. Our leader Ander and the rest know you have given us this. So, they'll remember that, which isn't bad for you or me."

Charista savored the compassion in Joanna's eyes. Joanna placed her hand on the screen as she said, "Dear, I promise you, I loved your father and made him a pledge that I'd watch out for you always, and that's what I'm going to do."

Chapter Five

C HARISTA'S SUMMONS ARRIVED two days after she returned. Her spirit sank when she saw the red digital document at the top of her incoming messages. It was there just when she'd thought she had a few days to not think about it. Breaking rank and sending the kind of comm Charista did would've earned any member of an Omegan flight crew time in port, admin leave without pay, a stint in Retooling, or worse. But, as Charista was already subject to reviews from her father's past, her latest deviance only added a healthy amount of fuel to that already blazing fire.

I just wish they'd give me a chance to breathe. How am I supposed to ever prove myself again if they're holding dad's past over me each waking moment?

As Charista fumbled with the manual controls that adjusted the light in the main room lower, a chime tone sounded on the viewscreen on her wall. Charista looked over to a report of the incoming haul of Xeno prisoners. *Maybe this will help my case. Of course, I'm sure By-the-Book Risberg will have his way with me on the insubordination charge.*

She flopped down into a chair. *Time to get ready for yet another grilling.*

* * *

After a fitful sleep, Charista woke up earlier than usual. She sprung out of bed, her mind chock full of ideas. This time, her schemes focused on her review. Charista imagined how her mother Winola prepared to lead troops into a skirmish. She also thought about her father, developing Brescar, steeped in the knowledge that any wrong step or move would've meant the end for him, probably planet Omegana and maybe even Ling Galaxy. Charista wasn't leading a skirmish, though, nor was she making complex calculations on an energy-producing matter that could've had drastic consequences.

Her battle was of the will. Her fighting arena was the Inquiry Hall. Her weapons: words. Those alone had enough power behind them, and she knew she had to be careful.

The Omegan Military escorts arrived promptly to pick her up. Once they put Charista in wrist restraints, they helped her into the transport for their ride to the center of town. The trip was mostly silent; the only noise in the cabin was the occasional chatter over the vehicle comm. Charista watched the Omegan buildings as they drifted past on their drive. Gajanan had many facilities for production and retooling, but the military was undoubtedly the most prominent presence there. The Science Wing had their collection of structures, too. Charista smiled as their vehicle passed the building where Findlay worked up until he was removed from his post. Despite Findlay's achievements in Omegan weapon power supplies and building structures like the one the *Trussel* crew installed on Agmon, his legacy, besides in the memories of Charista and Joanna, was betrayal.

The transport jolted to a stop. Charista glanced out the side window at the entrance to the Inquiry hall. Her two escorts exited first and helped Charista to the sidewalk at the bottom of the vast set of stairs leading into the hall. Several Omegans walked either up toward or down from the entrance. Amid the crowd, up ahead of them, Charista noticed one Omegan female in a military uniform covered with regal robes, facing Charista with a curious look on her face. As they climbed the steps, Charista caught more than a few glances from Omegans passing by in either direction. Omegans usually had no use for anyone in restraints. The common belief was that an Omegan in shackles was already guilty, especially given Charista being near the Inquiry hall.

As she got closer to the lone figure in the lavish uniform, Charista was relieved when she recognized their face.

Aunt Ardy.

Ardene Onopco was a high-ranking member of the Omegan Military. Furthermore, she served with Charista's mother and had been a close family friend for years. Growing up, Charista knew her as "Aunt Ardy."

When Charista and the guards were close enough, Ardene took a step closer. "Aside from the circumstances, it's great to see you."

Charista savored the relief of an unexpected familiar face. "Same here."

Ardene's face hardened to a steely military demeanor as she regarded Charista's escorts. "I'll take it from here. You two are dismissed."

The guards glanced at each other for a moment, then one grabbed Charista and pulled her to Ardene's step. Ardene clutched Charista as the two guards snapped a salute and exited.

Charista's arm throbbed from the guard's final grip on her, and she threw a glare back toward her former escorts, already on their way down to their vehicle.

"Omegan sentries are on the lower order of intelligence at the academy. They reserve the flight and advance combat assignments to those with more aptitude," Ardene said softly.

Charista took another look at Ardene's outfit. It wasn't field issue for Omegan Horde troops; instead, it was more ornate, with golden trim along the dark black tunic material. A formal outfit, used for ceremonies...

...and sometimes inquiry boards.

"Are you - on my review?" Charista asked.

Ardene leaned closer as they walked. "I am. Once I heard about you coming in, and what happened with you on the *Trussel*, I wanted to help."

I didn't realize insubordination would get around the Omegan military so quickly. I guess Aunt Ardy was keeping a closer eye on me. While the odds against her were still four to one at best, she felt better having someone with Ardene's chops in her corner.

Charista turned back to Ardene's warm grin. "Just so happens, the Xeno have become a hot topic over here since that stunt you pulled."

"I knew they were useful."

"Don't get ahead of yourself. Not much has changed on Omegans wanting to rule all of Ling since you've been away. But, there are cracks in the armor, and I understand several on your review board are interested in the Xeno. Some feel the Xeno could be weaponized, and it would be better to have them as an option than leaning too much on Malone for our goals. So, I'm bringing up the Xeno's value to Omegana in your review. Maybe we can deflect the discussion onto the value of what you did. Don't misunderstand; even if we can sell the Xeno's worth, you're still in for an awful assignment. But, if we keep you out of prison, I'll call that a win."

Charista's mind raced through possible arguments, but nothing stuck out to her. "I'm in a bad place, aren't I?"

"Afraid so. I've arranged to escort you to chambers while we wait for your hearing."

"How did you pull all this? I figured you'd be attacking UA headquarters on planet Yassel by now."

Ardene shrugged; a slight smirk found her face. "Zakmar owes me. He and Malone are deep into their love affair, working on the conquest of Ling. I just had to get away from those two for a bit.

Besides, I didn't want my favorite niece facing the dogs without a little protection." Ardene chuckled softly as they headed inside the hall.

* * *

Charista attempted a comfortable position in her seat but knew it was useless. Her chair faced a raised dais adorned with the Omegan crest, where five chairs held the board members reviewing her case. At an Omegan Review, the board didn't even remotely consider comfort for the one under examination. The Omegans wanted every discomfort possible in the hope the unease led to more chance revelations and damning bits of testimony that anyone in that much pain would've offered for some relief.

Once the proceedings began and after the list of charges was read to the assembled, Kai Risberg wasted no time going for the throat.

"She's a disgrace to the Omegana Crest! Insubordination from someone with the Mantisword's history of defiance deserves the maximum penalty!"

Risberg's assessment of Charista rang out in the ceremonial chamber. She winced at the sharp rebuke but noticed by their expressions that the Omegans present weren't as eager to support Kai's statement. Like many of the elder Omegans, Kai had become prone to a few slips of judgment himself, and the idea was brewing that Kai's time in active service, at least on a command level, was past the point where it made sense.

Nabarun Sule, presiding over the ceremonies, extended his hand toward Risberg in a silencing gesture. "The accused's crimes are noted, Captain Risberg. I agree her permissions with Tech need to be removed for an extended period. As to her ultimate penalty, this board will determine that in a short time." Sule was the Commandant at the Omegan Military Institute. Charista read the enjoyment on his face and wondered if that included a dismal outcome for her. She figured anyone steeped in training procedure also enjoyed the procedural side of the Omegan Machine.

After the opening barrage, Ardene strode about in the gap between Charista's table and the dais. "The accused is in review because of her father's history. There's no denying the severity of Ensign Mantisword's act of sending a comm transmission against orders, but let's consider for a moment what her actions gave Omegana: the Xeno. Our fight to overtake Ling Galaxy hasn't been without trouble. We've already lost several Horde units to UA forces. We don't have a clear path to victory. Our alliance with Malone has given us more teeth in the fight, but others are still biting us. We need to claw back. Remember our legacy, fellow Omegans... we are physically formidable, but might without strategy eventually falls flat. The truth is, we are at war, and in war, sometimes advantages make the difference between prevailing or not. There's plenty of debate over the value of the Xeno. Why don't we look at that for a moment, since this insubordination by Ensign Mantisword gave us an incoming asset?"

Risberg groaned in response. Charista figured Ardene could've named the exact color of the dais table, and Risberg would've objected. "General Onopco has chosen to deflect our discussions to the Xeno, using the topical subject of our recent acquisition. Let me make my feelings clear on this matter. I ordered Mantisword not to alert the Omegans about the Xeno convoy because I didn't want to waste time from Omegan operations. And, just because the incident we're discussing netted us a group of Xeno, it's no reason we should hold a collection of bastard outcasts from a distant galaxy as some great hope. Even if what we've heard is all true, and Xeno can wield Essence, that only makes them a threat in my eyes. We can exterminate them once they are housed on Omegana, for all I care. Xeno are simply a blight on what we are. Our scientific minds will realize that once they've had their time to poke and prod."

Synne Aren on the dais was another salty variety of Omegan old soldiers similar to Risberg. "What could a puny Xeno offer the likes of us? We are the supreme race in Ling Galaxy, are we not? We stand at a threshold of being the controlling force in Ling once we handle our ally Malone Stanton, that is."

Ardene glanced at Synne. "Malone has given Omegans a decent chance, but we shouldn't rule out the thought of Malone Stanton being removed one day. Omegans have had one master already with the Nara; the last thing we need is another with Stanton."

Nabaran smashed his gavel on the table, sending an echoed thud into the room. His voice boomed in the large hallway. "Malone Stanton isn't for debate here. We're all aware of the transgressions on the Mantisword name, and we've given extra attention to Ensign Mantisword's activities since. She's handled her duties with resolve, even the tiniest scrap repurpose detail, and we should consider that."

Kai retorted, "Oh, should we? What if we're under attack and need coordinates for assisting craft? Do we count on her to provide that information, or maybe she'll continue on this path? Who knows, maybe she's got some other connections."

"The truth, Captain Risberg," Nabarun offered, "Is while Ensign Mantisword was flagrant, her actions provided Omegana with the capture of the Xeno. Moreover, their apparent value to the UA makes them, at the very least, a bargaining chip for us. While their final worth is still up for debate, I appreciate the strategic nature of her insights."

"Well, that is only worthwhile if we can deem the Xeno have some use." Kai quipped.

Nabarun's eyes narrowed. His voice was steady and low when he spoke again. "I'm ordering the Science Wing to evaluate the Xeno, mentally and physically. We should at least rule out their abilities with Essence. As for the accused, she will be escorted back to chambers. Then, this board will decide the disposition of Charista Mantisword's case."

* * *

The board deliberated Charista's case for three hours. She paced back and forth in the small room that felt like a step above a prison cell. A lone seat stood in one corner, and on one wall was a monitor that flashed the Omegana crest.

I wish I could talk with Kindra or Adarsha. Just hugging them would be nice. It sounded like Aunt Ardy made some sense to the board. Who knows. Oh, when is this going to stop?

After what felt like a month for Charista, Ardene appeared. Charista searched her Aunt's face for any hints of how it went. Aunt Ardy was a seasoned warrior, though, and her demeanor held.

"Please tell me I'm not getting execution," Charista muttered.

"Not at all. It's a victory... of sorts. You're of course done with any starcraft assignments for a while. Risberg also wants nothing further to do with you. No surprise there."

"So, where am I going?"

"Supply service."

The words came like a slap across Charista's face. One of the minor assignments in Omegan society, the Supply Service dealt with lower order things like rations and part deliveries. It was an excellent place for someone who wanted to be forgotten, so Charista realized it was the prime choice for her sentence.

Charista felt Ardene's arm around her shoulder, and her voice was soft.

"Supply Service is better than Retooling, Charista."

"I think it's worse, Aunt Ardy. At least Retooling let me stretch my mind a little. Supply service means I'm a bonafide drone."

"And you've lost rank; you're back to officer candidate."

Charista shook her head. *Was there ever any end to all this?*

Charista leaned into Ardene's embrace, looking into her concerned eyes.

"Charista, listen. You're free. You're alive. That was my main goal. Just do what you're told. Omegana values loyalty, and yours will be much harder to prove for a while. It isn't impossible, but it's going to take time."

"What are the Omegans going to do with the Xeno?"

"I don't know. Omegana's attention to the scientific hasn't been the same since Findlay's death. Zakmar wants weapons, not innovation."

"But this is intelligence!" Charista felt like she was still in the inquiry and felt the pain as she looked into Ardene's eyes.

"Charista, pay your dues now; things will improve in time."

Charista sunk further into her seat. She knew Aunt Ardy was right. But, she also felt helpless, like any step she made forward was quickly erased with two to three steps back.

Chapter Six

THE OMEGAN DEPOT WAS A SHORT but wide building from which the Supply service delivered all the necessities throughout Omegana. Of course, those assigned to the service weren't envied for their jobs by members of the Omegan military or any other citizen. Still, the simple truth was that supply was the lifeblood of Omegana.

Charista's days in the Omegan Supply service became a blur, leaving her housing unit early to catch a transport to the Depot for her day's assignments, then running pieces of repurposed equipment from Retooling over to the Omegan Military wing.

Charista wasn't alone in her sentence, either. Isaac Pyatt, technically innocent of any involvement in Charista's Xeno comm transmission, but still complicit by the manner of being a supervisor over her, was given a temporary reassignment to the Omegan Supply Service. Charista figured it was collateral damage from her infraction.

Each day, Charista gathered in the large Depot main hallway to receive assignments for the day. The giant warehouse structure had a musty smell. Occasional dust wafts and the stale odor of smoke and random chemicals gave the place a very industrial feel. A fleet of transport vehicles lined one side of the large room. These were loaded for deliveries by several crews on hand. Charista fell in with the groups running deliveries, while the more experienced staff were relegated to sorting and organizing inventory for distribution.

Before the tasks began, there was often a group meeting where Griffen Nys, Captain of the Omegan Supply service, briefed the entire crew on the current demands of the Supply service. Griffen was the most detailed officer Charista had seen yet. His uniform was so impeccable, it made Isaac's look sloppy. Griffen strode back and forth, looking at his digital pad while Charista, Isaac, and the other assignees waited for his word.

"Omegana will rule Ling Galaxy one day. No true Omegan will dare debate that. But, we won't get there any quicker unless our nation is prepared. Our military has the strength, but it's up to us to keep the supply lines going, and that's what I expect of each of you. Now, the rules. No back talk. Several of you are here because you washed out somewhere else. If you thought this would be an easy assignment to work your way back, think again. Supply runs deliveries at all hours to Omegana. You'll work 15-hour shifts and like it, understood?"

"Yes sir!" Came the response from the assembled group.

One of the Supply Sergeants weaved through the crowd as the assembled workers pressed closer. Charista edged closer, but it wasn't much use. This was part of the daily routine. She wondered if the more aggressive in this surge of Omegan bodies got the more choice assignments.

The Supply Sergeant's eyes narrowed slightly when his gaze met Charista's. He flicked her orders over. Charista grabbed for the document as it smacked into her chest.

Charista grabbed the ticket and squirmed out of the pile to read the details.

Homestead. Great, I'm delivering rations or something.

Charista also noticed an additional assignee on her run. None other than Isaac. She glanced about until she saw him several yards away, eyeing a similar document. Without making visual contact with Isaac, she glanced back to the transports and matched the vehicle number with her orders. *Maybe if I leave fast enough, I can ditch him.*

Unfortunately, Isaac met Charista when she was almost to the vehicle.

"Don't think for a Tausian minute I've forgotten what happened. You better believe I will do everything possible to make your life a living hell until I get out of here."

Charista narrowed her eyes. "Suck it up, Isaac. I'm sure you'll weasel out of this in no time."

* * *

Charista and Isaac's run took most of the day to complete. Afterward, they returned to the Depot. The warehouse, filled with vehicles and Omegans in the early part of the day, stood half empty, like a mother animal waiting for her young's return. Charista parked their vehicle alongside the few others back in the hall and headed toward the rear of the depot, where crews of more senior Supply workers handled the incoming materials for future deliveries.

After a few minutes, Charista caught sight of Edin and motioned him toward the rows of parked transports.

"So," Edin began, "What's your plan for Brescar?"

Charista swiped at her brow. The temperature in the depot was always much warmer than the outside. The continual traffic of large transport vehicles in and out spewed enough rancid exhaust to keep the place pretty stuffy and warm.

"The Horde shipments are leveling off. I think you'll be able to grab one of those freighters soon. Just put a small amount in for now. We don't need any more attention than we already have."

Edin nodded.

"Tell me again, how much Brescar is left?"

"My last count came to 30 cases, each with approximately two tons of Brescar."

Charista marveled. Joanna was probably going to get Replication figured out anyway, but having that large a supply still around was nice. Her main concern was how long Edin's story of disposal to hide his shipments of Brescar to Joanna held up with the Omegan authorities.

At the end of one day, Charista noticed a group of Supply workers watching a large video screen in the Warehouse. The Xeno were brought in and received by Zakmar himself.

I guess they want to study the Xeno before mutilating them after all. At least getting busted for pointing out their convoy wasn't for nothing.

After the initial reception, the Xeno were brought to the Omegan prison with as much fanfare as the delivery of fabricated building components. She eyed her display tablet that showed a rough count of the individuals in the group. There wasn't time for more detailed information, but she was ready to find that out herself.

Chapter Seven

CHARISTA'S ROUTINE IN SUPPLY SERVICE gave way to drudgery. The days ran to weeks, and while she thought about her plans, they seemed to drift into a daydream. She even got better at tuning out Isaac's bickering. Nevertheless, her tasks continued to be as menial as she could've imagined, running food rations and checking on the supply relays for power converters.

One day, the mundane stopped abruptly. It began with the sound of weapons fire as Charista and Isaac were on one of their regular runs. At first, she thought it was a weapons test. But as it continued, given its location, she knew it wasn't a drill. The noise came from the Prison area, and the sight of UA ships further confirmed what she thought.

Then, a mysterious comm entry over their vehicle's speakers.

"Requesting assistance from Omegana security, Prison under attack, repeat, prison under attack."

Charista met Isaac's gaze, his eyes filled with bewilderment.

"Could that be a drill?" Charista asked.

Isaac frowned a bit and eyed the comm speaker. "I can't imagine why they'd do that at the prison."

Charista grabbed the comm and replied. "Omegana Prison, please repeat; sounded like you said you're under attack?"

"Affirmative. It looks like an attempted prison break."

Charista accessed the video feed of the detention building on their vehicle's console. Sure enough, a collection of UA ships and troops battered the area. She slammed her fist on her thigh, angry about Omegan carelessness over home defense, especially regarding a valuable asset.

While Isaac wrung his hands, Charista felt the gears in her strategic mind slip back into place. *Of course, the UA saw enough in the Xeno to grab them first; why wouldn't they have risked a mission to the Omegan stronghold?*

Charista smashed her hands together. "Isaac, we have to help them."

"With what? We've got a load of medical supplies."

"There's weapons at the prison. Our fellow Omegans are in trouble. What about the Omegan credo about 'No Omegan forsakes another'?"

"That's fine talk from a Mantisword." Isaac eyed Charista with a deep snarl.

"A Mantisword who's trying to do the right thing and save other Omegans right now. Are you helping, or should I report you ignored Omegans under siege?"

Isaac gnashed his teeth, his eyes glaring at the unfolding scene on the monitor. "Damn it, OK."

Charista flung the vehicle in gear and headed toward the prison building. She craved a battle for several reasons. First, it was ingrained in Omegans, given their desire for absolute rule. Bloodlust was bred and fostered in their kind for centuries. Second, the chance at action after weeks of a painfully dull routine felt like the best medicine she could've gotten.

Once Charista and Isaac arrived at the Prison, they met a small force of Omegans that scurried around with pulse rifles toward defensive positions for the oncoming attack. After a few minutes, Charista found Jamon, the warden. He was a burly hulk of an Omegan. He looked about at the rush of troops with an agitated gaze, but once his eyes met Charista's, a sneer found his face.

"Well, if it isn't the Traitor."

Aaand they know me here too. Figures.

Isaac spoke next. "Captain, we heard your distress call. Unfortunately, we don't have much in arms, but we're here to assist however we can."

Jamon glanced over to Isaac and nodded. "We could always throw this one toward the ships."

Really? They're about to be blown up, and they still don't want my help?

The ground rocked with a series of blasts. Charista steadied herself against a nearby wall. Jamon's voice lifted to a decibel level of an Omegan training instructor. "Troops to the outside embankments and put fire on the craft. Those on interior security fortify the holding levels. Keep those prisoners safe. We lose so much as one; You'll all pay for it!"

Charista and Isaac joined the remaining officers in getting weapons. Charista grabbed a helmet and proceeded outside toward the forward defensive positions. The evening air was dry, with a slight warm breeze coming. A series of UA small fighters swarmed the skies above.

Jamon strode about as Charista and the others crouched behind the elevated embankment, their pulse rifles trained on the approaching ships. "We know what's here; I want to know what's coming and how big our threat is."

An officer with a head visor tapped the controls and gazed directly at the inbound craft. "Another cluster en route. Large Transport or two, with several small fighters."

"They're not an attack unit," Jamon muttered. "There'd be at least a few cruisers in there. They were hoping for a snatch and grab."

"The Xeno," Charista offered.

"Brilliant deduction," Jamon countered. "Well, they're ours, and they're staying here, understood?"

Shouts of confirmation and the telltale whir sound of rifles powered up answered Jamon's call like an eager congregation.

The collective group of Omegans on hand numbered fifty, with no starcraft support. Whatever was about to happen was sure to include a slaughter of Omegans. Charista knew what she would've done if she had a say, but remembered how acting quick in the past wasn't her best move.

"Sir, maybe Omegana can send support?" Charista asked.

Jamon glared in response. "I've already called them, Officer Candidate. What do you think that comm was for? Omegan military is scrambling what they can to give us reinforcements."

Several blasts from the approaching starcraft peppered the ground nearby. Jamon took an angry swipe of his brow. "I'm heading to the command tower. It's not much, but it's got the best vantage point and a few guns. At least we can throw more fire on the UA from there."

Isaac edged up onto his feet. "Sir, I have experience with anti-ship weaponry. I can assist."

Jamon's mouth curled. "Can't hurt at this point, come on."

Charista shook her head as Isaac trotted off behind Jamon like a loyal pet. *You do have a way of weaseling up to whatever CO is nearby, don't you?*

Her attention returned to the fray, Charista steadied her weapon. Her fellow officers were also there to her right and left, ready. They waited quietly, but she noticed the look in her fellow troop's eyes: heightened readiness.

Blasts from the smaller craft lanced the ground. Charista wobbled in her position while dust rained from the overhead canopy. *They'll send the small ships in for us. The transport won't have a lot of weapons; they're more worried about loading up the prisoners there. If we keep a low profile, we can hit them when they start to leave.*

Three of the small starcraft shot in an arch formation on a direct course for the platform where Charista and her group waited. A barrage of pulse fire shot up the embankment. The structure shook violently on the impact.

Charista winced as the metal around them heated up. The craft flew past and seemed to disappear, but Charista knew better. "They're coming back around. This unit won't stand much more than that. We've gotta move!"

The firing on their position stopped. Charista glanced up and saw why. The craft swiveled their course into a path toward the command tower. The guns from the building were small, but they peppered the starcraft for all they were worth. But it wasn't enough, and the three craft launched a volley of missiles that slammed into the tall structure with a cacophony of explosions. Charista and her fellow trench mates were knocked to the ground. When she looked up again, the former tower lay on its side, a mixture of mangled structural pieces and fires.

After the first wave of panic hit Charista, she felt her nerves calm, and the warrior spirit of her mother took over. "Take cover!"

She barked the words with such authority; the rest around her followed without question.

Charista stood up quickly. Her visor filled with dirt, but she was at least out of the hulking target of a defensive position she'd been in moments earlier. She noticed in the darkness a few others had taken her up on her move. She held her rifle up and pointed to an outcropping in the near distance.

An Omegan to Charista's right shouted, "Over there! Service connection. We can get behind it until reinforcements get here!"

It wasn't the best circumstances, but even in that brawl, she saw something. It wasn't her fellow soldiers huddled for cover. Instead, it was a hand terminal clipped to the waist of a fallen Omegan that lay face down in the debris. Charista grabbed the device, flipped through screens until the display showed controls of the facility, and pulled up the security recording. The system was designed to report any breaks or at least attempted breaks, but the video would've captured the assault and, more so, what was done by the Omegans who defended the place.

As other Omegans around fired on the UA craft that swarmed about, Charista weaved and stumbled over the pieces of the destroyed tower. While the structure lay on its side, she thought maybe the top portion was still there. If nothing else, the auto-destruct for the base should've been easier to find if she had started from the central tower.

A wall of flames lapped at her legs, and she scooted back, her feet rolling on a busted pipe that protruded from the ground. She went through a broken window and found herself inside the command center. A few bodies were scattered over the floor. She smirked at the sight of Isaac's body, unconscious. Jamon was nearby. His frame was covered with multiple cuts, and trails of darkish gray blood oozed from several places on his body, including his mouth. Still, he had a comm in his hand.

"Where's that damned backup?"

Charista saw the expression on Jamon's face, and instantly, she felt something. It wasn't compassion but a bit of recognition. Jamon was in a panic, and Charista savored the helplessness. *See, that's what it's like when you're in a tough spot. You've all kept me in one for a while now. Now it's your turn.*

As the chaos continued, Charista's thoughts rose above the conflict as a plan shot into her mind. It was more than a comm sent against orders; it was even more than her father or mother's attempts to improve their situation. Charista had a role in this attack, and it was that of a savior. But it was a story she had to write, and she had details to arrange.

Charista's hand squeezed the handle of her pulse rifle tight, and she held the weapon across her shoulders, behind her back as she stood.

Jamon's voice was a rasp, mixed with the blood that now gurgled in his throat. "Get down. Are you crazy? They can still obliterate this place and all of us, including you!"

While Jamon had focused on the next move at hand, Charista had already looked ahead in the game - her game. And, a play materialized. It was a bold one, but completely smart. It was even necessary given where she wanted to be.

So, Charista ignored Jamon's warning. She was still very much aware of the fight but suddenly realized she had an option. One maybe she'd had earlier and hadn't taken, but this time, she knew what she had to do.

Charista flung her rifle to a ready position in a single motion and fired several volleys into Jamon's chest. His body jerked violently as it broke into warm pieces of flesh as blood cascaded around it. She waited for a few moments until Jamon's gurgling heaves stopped. She then edged herself closer to Isaac. He hadn't budged since she entered the busted tower. *No sense in leaving anything to chance; I'll never get this good an opportunity again with the fight outside masking anything in here.*

As the pulse shots sliced Isaac's body into an unrecognizable pile of flesh, a surge of power went through Charista. Some of it was payback, some was power, but most of all, she felt more justification than she could've ever imagined.

When it was over, Isaac and Jamon's bodies lay in a heaped pile. Then, after what seemed like several hours passed, Jamon's comm crackled to life.

"Omegan Air Support Unit with visual on bandits, contacting ground crew, anyone there?"

Charista yanked the comm from Jamon's dead hand. "Charista Mantisword - they slaughtered our CO, but there's a few of us left, get some fire on those ships ASAP!"

* * *

Charista made it outside in time to see Omegan starcraft mopping up the remains of the failed UA rescue attempt. She saw one UA fighter burst into a brilliant explosion. The Transport had pulled away, and the other UA Craft engaged the Omegan ships as they beat their retreat.

Charista met with a group of Omegan support troops, who eyed her with concern. She noticed the lieutenant insignia on the one to the front and observed the name embossed on their uniform breast pocket: Garton Hammon. The annoyed glare on his face told her the best move was for short answers and a wide berth.

"Where's Jamon?" Hammon's question came out like an order.

"Dead. I helped him contact Omegana military, and that's all he was able to do."

"We have to check for survivors. There could be more in that rubble." Hammon eyed the crumbled structure.

Charista nodded. "Understood, sir. We still have a substantial asset below: the Xeno. I recommend we load them out ASAP before the UA doubles back with more ships."

Chapter Eight

WITH THE HELP OF THE OMEGANA MILITARY, Charista and the surviving detail soldiers were pulled out, and the Xeno prisoners were relocated into the Science Wing facilities. The incident was relayed back to Omegan command, and Charista was heralded a hero for her actions. She bristled with the praise while wondering if she'd covered her tracks as well as she thought she had. Charista had taken a significant step forward, though, and that was good enough for now.

With help from her old friend Edin, they grabbed one of the damaged UA starcraft, and Edin worked out a deal to repurpose the ship for another delivery of Brescar. It was a short-term fix, but Charista was grateful for the extra time to figure out how to get the supply chain to Joanna restored for good.

Charista had made her move the right way and was assigned to a combat unit. She knew she had the best chance to be seen for her skill and eventually begin the rise up the ranks required for her eventual coup.

Entering the Science Wing felt odd for Charista since her father's death. In his former workplace, she felt good, being near to at least his spirit, but the betrayal that went with the Science Wing was the other side of that picture. Once she got to the holding area for the Xeno, she was met with a small but decently armed group of Omegan soldiers. A simple flash of her credentials was all it took, and she was escorted inside.

That's right; I'm Officer Candidate Mantisword no more.

Charista met Sergeant Hussey Ganesh at the observation desk. After a moment, the sergeant's face showed recognition of Charista, and his mouth formed a line.

"Ensign Mantisword, how can I help you?"

Charista glanced past the desk down the hallway, where two Omegan guards strode toward the far end. "I'm here to evaluate the Xeno prisoners. I understand their processing hasn't started yet, so I'd like to do some of my own checking."

Ganesh glanced up the hallway, then back. His eyes widened a bit. Clearly, there were no plans for the Xeno, but again, the Omegan priorities left the collection of prisoners to more or less rot away for the time being. "I suppose you can have a pass through, but don't take too much-"

"-thank you, Sergeant. I'll mention this to your shift commander when I'm done."

Charista pulled a hand terminal from the rack to the side of the desk while Ganesh opened access for her to the inner holding area.

Private Wosley Prior led Charista down into the holding area. The Omegan battle armor heavily accented his medium build. He strode with his rifle to his side, a mildly disinterested glint in his eye. After a few twists and turns down the corridors, Charista found herself walking along a row of cells.

"I can't figure out why we keep these nasty Xeno here. They're an infection if ya ask me. They probably started Veculus, ya know."

Charista nodded. *Grunt, I don't need your amateur analysis.*

The Xeno faces were a mosaic of moods, ranging from desperate and sad to irritated and angry. The hall was thick with the pungent odor of bodies that hadn't been cleaned in some time. The yellowish overhead lights added a slight burning scent to the air.

"Are any of these military?" Charista asked Wosley while she scanned her terminal for any information. The data appeared to be pretty straightforward, a headcount, not much more. Nevertheless, she hoped the guard had picked up some good old-fashioned intel.

Wosley frowned and offered a mild chuckle. "I dunno. They were all on that transport, mixed together. A few of 'em tried making trouble, but we shut that down right quick. They probably had warriors in the lot; not sure how many survived, though."

Charista stopped at one of the cells, where an adult female gazed blankly at her. Charista's eyes met the Xeno's, their long black hair was tousled, but their piercing stare was striking. Charista glanced back to Wosley. "I think I'm good here. I'll check a few of them out and call you when I'm done."

"Fine with me." Wosley already started back up the hallway, only slowing to add, "There's no bounty on these, and I'm getting tired of wading through their scummy mess. You wanna do a few of them in; I won't notice."

After a few moments, the heavy door at the end of the hallway clanged shut, and the rattle reverberated through the hallways. Then, Charista was back studying the Xeno. She recognized a UA symbol on her uniform and figured her initial instinct was right. Charista eyed the profiles of the Xeno until she matched the face with a file in her records.

"Selina... Ravencraft?"

Selina said nothing but glanced back at her accommodations. The rest of the Xeno looked more or less docile. Many hadn't worn any outfits that screamed military or even aggressors. But, in Omegana's eyes, they were all subjects, and the more she got from them, the better for her own sake.

"Listen, Selina. You probably think you shouldn't help me at all, but if you give me a chance, I think you'll find I can help you."

Selina's eyes slowly worked back to Charista's. Charista smiled a little, feeling like she'd at least made a crack in the facade.

"According to my records here, you were one of the leaders of this group."

Selina kept quiet but eyed Charista through a pair of eyes stained with annoyance and anger. "Guess that's the rumor."

Charista nodded. "I know you've been through a lot, and I know you're probably not sure why you're even with us."

Selina stared at Charista. "I'm guessing all that commotion when we were moved here wasn't exactly the plan?"

"Your friends at the UA tried to rescue you, but in their usual way, they underestimated the situation before they jumped into it."

"Mmhmm."

"I can help you, but I need to know you'd be interested in helping me."

Selina arched a brow. "Does it involve us going free?"

"It could."

"Are we supposed to join you or something?"

"It's not quite that simple." Charista took a slow breath and offered a smile. "The truth is, I'm fascinated by your kind. You don't want to be here. My people don't even really want you here, other than it gets you out of their way. But I'm interested. Ellene Ballo seems to think you can control Essence. So, maybe we can help each other."

"Why don't you ask her then?"

"That's just it; she's vanished. We're unsure where to find her."

"Yeah? Guess we can't help you out there... too bad."

Charista shrugged. "Selina, you can be upset about your situation, but until you realize the galaxy doesn't owe you unless you contribute to it first, you'll never rise above the mealy state your kind has perpetually been in."

Selina slammed the walls of her cell. The electropulse responded with a loud twang noise and sent a shock into Selina's hand. She yelped and pulled her hand back from the wall, which glowed bright red at the spot she'd hit.

"Selina, don't do that again. These can hold much bigger things than your kind."

Selina only offered an annoyed glare in response.

Charista realized convincing Selina involved more than just some well-aimed words. "How about we take a walk? I'll show you a few things we're trying here, and you can decide just how important it is you work with us or not?"

Charista saw the Xeno as a chance that hadn't been wasted. She'd made it to the next step despite all she'd faced, overzealous superior officers, reviews, and orders to avoid the Xeno at all costs. What came afterward was unclear, but she had found her footing again, and her next step wasn't too far away.

COLLATERAL CRISIS

Chapter One

S ELINA RAVENCRAFT WAS BACK at NewEarth for two days and already knew the colony was ancient history. No clairvoyance was required for that assessment; the community of humans on planet Zormad had seen far better times. Selina stood on top of the former ark ship *Intrepid* and watched the chaos that was, until recently, the colony of NewEarth, her home. At least the *Intrepid* was already broken down. The rest of NewEarth was recently ravaged by a unit of marauding Railen, just one of the collateral effects of an intergalactic conflict spreading further into Ling Galaxy.

"Hey Selina, where y'at?"

Warrah Malek's voice over the comm gave Selina a welcome pause from the lurid landscape. "I'm on the *Intrepid* wreckage, checking the scene. What's up?"

"Oh, just pinging you. Thought you might have been with the Nara on their ship."

Selina gazed over at the *Dionysus*. It wasn't quite the size of the *Intrepid* but bigger than a cruiser. The blue steel starcraft was as much a mystery as a standout, a pristine oblong sphere amid a sea of chaos and devastation.

"Yeah, no. Like they'd let a dirty Xeno on there with the Hierarch."

Warrah chuckled. "Well, I've heard Zed wants you to meet with Ellene."

"Oh yeah, and just where'd you hear that from, Ms. Malek?"

After a few moments of silence, Warrah giggled.

"What, does Ramsey talk in his sleep?"

Ramsey Nock was one of the most notorious trainers in the Regulation. While many found him imposing, Warrah was drawn to his outward strength, and the two became an item not long after Selina and Warrah became active troops in the Regulation.

Warrah finally found her composure. "Hey, Zed keeps his cadre up to speed, and that's not just you, Ms. Ravencraft."

"All I know is Zed wants me to shadow Ellene, and in a million years, I'll never understand why."

"Whatever the reason, don't forget us little people when you're big and famous."

Selina laughed out loud, a guffaw that she desperately needed. Warrah was one of Selina's oldest friends from the Regulation. The bond they forged in training was a tonic for Selina, especially in chaotic times.

"Well, don't take too long up there."

Selina sighed deeply. "I won't. See you in a few."

Plumes of black smoke dotted the scene, from housing areas to the NewEarth Council building, and even Ward's Commissary. The once popular gathering place for NewEarth residents was sliced nearly in two by Railen armaments during the skirmish.

While the reason for the Railen attack remained a mystery to many, Selina knew why they came. She clutched the Disruptor device, a small cylinder, against her thigh in its hiding place as she walked down into NewEarth. Had it not been for Selina's last-minute abduction during the Railen attack, she may have lost the device, and her life like several Regulation troopers did.

The air was filled with a thick sour smell. While the attack happened two days prior, the fires had only begun to die out. A group of Regulation troops passed Selina, carrying another litter of bodies from a former residence on NewEarth. Each new sight of remains gave Selina a grim feeling.

A flash of light hit Selina's eye. Once the momentary glare passed, she looked in the direction where it came. There was the *Crimson Lance*, her one-time ride. The freighter coughed steam from various ports while Ket Durban worked on some access panels with help from W915, or "Dub," his robot assistant.

Instead of being in the thick of the Railen attack, Selina was yanked off-world and onto Ket's ship. At the time, it was because of a Railen Tracker she had on herself. Ket was out for the tracker only, but the situation parlayed into an arrangement: Selina's return to Zormad for getting the tracker to settle a bounty he'd accepted.

Ket made good on his promise, returning Selina to Zormad. Selina also stuck to her guns, namely the Tracker Ket drooled over, and kept it on herself until she'd set foot back on Zormad. Since their return, Ket quickly fixated on his next move, which had absolutely nothing to do with the salvage of NewEarth. Selina knew the smuggler had his payday in mind, and the cargo he carried did no good for him as long as he stayed on Zormad. *You would think the creep would look around and stay a while to help, but whatever.*

Selina arched her back in a pointless attempt at getting the knots out but gave up after a few tries. Unfortunately, the soreness and throbbing were there to stay. The discomfort was collateral damage on her body for the swift moves she and the Regulation had taken with everything that happened in a short time.

A collection of Regulation troops met Selina as she got to the beginning of the former housing areas of NewEarth. Citizens milled around, many working on clearing their housing units out, so there were plenty of jobs to which Selina could direct soldiers. The feeling of troops following Selina around, several of which were older than her, was odd, but she pushed beyond that to do what was necessary.

Her father Erick, one of the first humans to ever set foot on Zormad, did so much to get NewEarth started that Selina felt pain at the colony's current state. She imagined her father nearby, giving comfort in his presence.

Selina's status on NewEarth quickly went from up-and-coming graduate to kidnapped to a leadership role within the Regulation. Jared, Selina's supervisor, was one of many casualties of the Railen attack, along with other Regulation commanders. Zed survived and moved quickly to pull up those best qualified. Given the situation, "alive and breathing" was an essential prerequisite.

A rancid smell hit Selina's nose, and she realized she'd gotten close to the pile of human bodies, recovered from the attack. The remains were brought toward the outskirts of NewEarth, where several left tokens, small notes, and mementos of their lost loved ones. The makeshift memorial site was a grim reminder of what the survivors truly lost in the attack.

A burst of warm planet Zormad air kissed Selina's face as she wiped the thin layer of sweat from her brow. In addition to Selina and Zed, the council of NewEarth survived to a degree. It regrouped fast, quickly brokering a deal for migration into the nearby city of Tas Ralong, in hope the reduced visibility within the Mardak city lessened or even dropped the target on NewEarth's back. The Mardaks, residents of Zormad for centuries before humans arrived, built a relationship with the NewEarth group over time. The Railen attack helped to cement the bond further.

Among the scenes of disaster mitigation, a long and snaking line of humanity had begun forming toward Tas Ralong. Landcrawlers, large trucklike vehicles of NewEarth, helped to a point. But, the refugees desperate to get to safety gave way to a hasty migration in any way possible, mostly on foot.

A few shouts caught Selina's attention, and she saw Warrah stooping over a pile of debris with several other Regulation officers.

Selina froze and debated looking away. Unfortunately, sights like that often meant another corpse found in the rubble, but thankfully, it was a few crates of food stores.

Warrah's group was moving their find onto a landcrawler when Selina walked up.

"How goes it?" Selina asked.

Warrah shrugged. "We found a few days of food, which is at least something."

"Yep."

Once the ration box was loaded, Warrah joined Selina for a quick walk around the scene. What remained of the housing units was quickly being broken into piles of valuable items among a sea of charred and mangled trash. Whenever Selina thought she had adjusted to the sight of so much debris, she got another shock of a once familiar location from NewEarth reduced to a pile of rubble beyond recognition.

Selina managed a nervous cough and looked about, but she soon felt Warrah's hand on her arm.

"Hey... you OK?"

Selina wanted to blame the smoke for the tears in her eyes. Warrah slid her arm across Selina's shoulders. "I know. We're all in this together, don't worry about a thing."

"Oh, I've got plenty to worry about."

"Well, you're an officer now."

Selina sighed. "I'm an officer because I didn't get wasted like the rest were." Selina knew, at least in part, there was nothing she could've done. She had no say in being nabbed from the Railen attack by Ket. But the whirlwind of being back on Zormad in the middle of the demolished NewEarth and her elevated role left her mind spinning for answers.

"I gotta check on Ward. Gonna be a lot of mouths to feed still, so Ward's got to be up and running soon to handle that."

Warrah nodded. "I'll keep on with the clean-up. Don't worry. We'll be back to schooling these Regulation guys in no time."

The two friends shared a small chuckle and tight embrace before they parted. Selina next headed toward the Commissary, where Ward Dixon watched a group from NewEarth dismantling his building. The large sign that once hung over the main entrance was among the destroyed parts. The colored and lighted marker was a familiar and comforting symbol not just of NewEarth, but the restaurant signage of the Earth humans left behind decades earlier.

Ward's eyes were heavy as he watched his place like a worried parent. Selina stood next to him for a while before he spoke.

"They were after us for something, weren't they?"

Ward's face was still fixed, his eyes tarnished with fear. Selina slid her arm across his back. "Yeah."

"I don't understand - why kill us? What the hell made us deserve this? I don't get it."

Several yards away, a Regulation trooper appeared from the command center. The structure, like most around NewEarth, had seen better days, but the Regulation kept its use up until the move to Tas Ralong was complete

As Selina watched the Regulation officer make their way over to the housing unit, Selina's mind returned to Ward. *I should tell Ward about the Disruptor. It was dad's, but I'm the one who had it when the Railen returned for it. That's why they attacked. But, if I tell him, he'll know who has the Disruptor too, making him more vulnerable if they return.*

"Ward, the Railen are just out to make trouble. I've heard on Network they do this all over Ling."

Network, otherwise known as the consolidated collection of comm transmissions throughout Ling Galaxy, was a mash-up in many unhelpful ways. However, it was also the best way to glean any helpful information about movements in Ling Galaxy, provided you took the time to filter out the sprawling array of transmission threads.

Ward nodded. "I forget you listen to that Network jumble."

They stood in silence again. Selina knew, as important as places like the Commissary were to talk, laugh, and share in good times, the support NewEarth citizens showed each other in bad patches made NewEarth a lasting community.

More wafts of smoke made Selina's nose itch, and before long, she busted into a coughing fit. Then it was Ward's turn to soothe her.

"You don't have to wait with me, Selina. You better check on the ones who got it worse."

Selina nodded, glancing back at the burning pile of corpses. "We'll all be in Tas Ralong soon."

"You say that like you don't think it's a good idea."

"There's no other option right now. That doesn't make Tas Ralong the right move. What's so different over there, besides bigger buildings? The Railen know we're around, and we're an easy target. It won't take much for them to come back."

Selina's vision suddenly clouded with tears, but she knew it wasn't the smoke this time. Selina's mother Laurina was one of the casualties of the attack. The sting had only begun to set in, and she found herself ravaged by waves of grief randomly in between bouts of frantic work to help with the salvage and relocation efforts.

She felt a nudge and looked up into Ward's compassionate eyes.

"She was a good woman, Selina. She won't be forgotten."

Selina nodded wordlessly, tears flicking from her face as Ward pulled her into a tight embrace. No words would've better filled the silence. Selina needed a moment, and Ward was happy to allow her that.

Ward spoke gently into their embrace. "We'll get through this."

Selina only managed an emotional "Mmmhmm."

* * *

Feeling slightly more composed, Selina said her goodbyes to Ward as she watched the movements of troops gathering pieces of NewEarth for the move. She'd waited long enough. Ket and Dub's work on the *Crimson Lance* had finished. While the idea of him sticking around was ridiculous to her, the more stubborn part of Selina figured it was worth one more attempt.

She neared Ket as he closed an exterior access panel underneath the *Crimson Lance* fuselage.

"So, you're really leaving?"

Ket's eyes lit for a moment at the sound of Selina's voice, and then a world-weary smirk took over his expression. "I gotta make good on this payday. If I don't come through, I've some pretty nasty threats against me."

"Ket, come on. You've seen what's going on here. We're short on help right now and could use a good pilot like you. You gonna chase paydays the rest of your life?"

Ket whistled, and Selina heard the whirrs of Dub's propulsion system behind her. "You just need to dig in deeper, and it looks like you're doing that. What do you need a flyer for?"

Selina noticed a lot about Ket in her short time with him beyond a stark portrait of his bravado. He was brash and bold and had a way of working through problems, especially the lethal kind. However, Selina caught glimpses of someone else beneath that tough and sometimes arrogant exterior: someone warm and caring. Selina was unconscious when Ket took her aboard the *Crimson Lance*, and he could've easily killed her. But Ket didn't. As they returned to Zormad, Selina realized she felt something toward the smuggler. Still, it remained unsaid between them. Selina hadn't felt an attraction to anyone since adulthood. She'd mainly worried about living in and moving out of the shadow of her father's legacy. The idea of sharing anything besides a Regulation assignment with someone hadn't come up on her radar until Ket.

Selina stifled a gasp when Ket clasped her shoulders. His greenish eyes peered deeply into hers, and Selina froze. "Look, you've got my contact token. You can call whenever you want."

"You'll be on the far side of the galaxy in a few days anyway." Selina glanced offward, unconcerned about the wounded tone in her voice.

Ket leaned in, and his voice softened. "Selina, I gotta do this. It's what I am."

She nodded and backed up from his grasp, noticing Dub to her side. "Take care of this maniac for me, will ya?"

Dub glanced to Ket and back to Selina. "Don't I always?"

Selina managed a polite yet fake smile and turned from the two. Almost as quickly as their paths crossed, they diverged. Selina felt a sting of the separation, but the loss was just one more for her, and she had to brace herself to continue the important job of saving the rest of her people who survived and were determined to stay.

Chapter Two

S ELINA HAD BARELY LEFT the *Crimson Lance* when she heard a voice to her right.

"Selina, a word?"

Ellene Ballo, Hierarch of the Nara, came to Zormad a day after Selina's return. The Mardaks verified Ellene as who she claimed to be, but even a confirmation like that wasn't enough for Selina. Ellene was a two-part mystery. The first was why the leader of the Nara, a prominent race in Ling Galaxy, was suddenly so interested in humans. The second was why Selina was suddenly ordained caretaker of Ellene during her visit to NewEarth.

While Zed and the rest of the leadership focused on the migration to Tas Ralong, Zed had Selina talk with Ellene. The assignment bugged her, and at the moment with Ellene trailing her, her irritation percolated.

Selina strode down the rows of housing units while Ellene walked beside her.

I'm not a diplomat. That was my dad's thing, Zed. "I'm not sure what I'm supposed to say to you, Ms. Ballo."

"Please, call me Ellene. Look, Selina. I know you and your people are in a world of pain right now."

"What clued you in, the pile of bodies?"

"I'm here to tell you I can help your people survive and regain your stature, even ascend to a greater one."

NewEarth never had polished and perfect residential districts, even in its best state. But for Selina, until a few days ago, it was home. Seeing so many buildings destroyed, with many more on fire or in severe disrepair, shook Selina to her core and had her in full-on fight mode.

Selina strained to keep the tremble out of her voice while holding onto that air of command she figured everyone expected from her. "Ellene, a third of our population is dead, including my mom. Most of our buildings are ruined, or at the very least, need serious repair. I've got a lot to keep track of, so I'm a little busy now."

A quick burst of warm air swept past, fluttering Ellene's flowing hair. The Nara were stewards of Essence, the life-giving substance to Ling Galaxy, but that was all Selina knew about them. All the suffering that hit NewEarth in just minutes made Selina wonder what Essence was worth since it hadn't prevented the colony's destruction.

"Selina, I'm truly sorry about your mother. And, the rest of your dead - what the Railen did is horrible. But, they want to rule this galaxy and don't care who or what they destroy to do it."

Selina bit her lip to stifle a cry. She didn't know why at the time, but something in her mind said to hold firm because showing Ellene any more emotion than she already had would've weakened her in Ellene's eyes. Selina's eyes closed as she spoke slowly, her voice straining to contain her emotions. "Why attack defenseless people? We weren't strong enough to face the Railen when we did. It's only blind luck that kept them from killing everyone here."

Selina felt Ellene's hand on her shoulder.

"Selina, the Railen and Omegans only succeed when fear thrives. The more they scare everyone, the better for them. It's not necessarily about what you have. You want safety for your people; it's what anyone reasonable would want. What if I offered you and your people accommodation in the safest place in Ling Galaxy?"

Selina looked into Ellene's thoughtful eyes. "Where exactly is a 'safe place'?"

"Planet Yassel, headquarters of the UA. They've got good defenses and always have a garrison on hand. You'll be near the seat of the UA government and president Nic Sava. It's the best place you could be right now."

Planet Yassel, central in Ling Galaxy, seemed almost mythical in the descriptions Selina heard of it. She imagined shimmering cities of colossal towers, where the population led the good life. The mental pictures were equally glamorous and frustrating, given how far life on Zormad was from that ideal.

Selina turned toward a crew clearing one of the housing units. The three covered bodies near the front of the property said plenty about the outlook there. Selina swung her boot at the ground, sending a spray of crumbled soil toward Ellene. "Where were you when we were under attack? We could've used you then."

"I know, and I'm sorry." Ellene's eyes met Selina's with a sad look. "This conflict has stretched our abilities far more than ever. I hope you realize that while we failed in helping some of your people, I'm here now to prevent this from happening again to more of you."

"Ellene, as tempting leaving Zormad sounds right now, our council makes decisions like this. If they decide you're for real, they'll still have to bring this to a vote among our people. That's how we make decisions, and Ellene, we're short on trust right now. Mardaks are our most reliable option."

Ellene nodded. "The Mardaks are certainly rugged. Their survival in these conditions with little outside assistance is a fine testament. Be that as it may, your presence here has roused the attention of more than just the Railen. I'm afraid more trouble is headed this way soon. If I'm right, even your partnership with the Mardaks won't stop further bloodshed."

A series of shouts interrupted their conversation. A crew of Regulation troops and regular citizens was in the middle of bringing down a partially demolished building, and its structural pieces had shifted dangerously. "Ellene, we have to get to shelter before more trouble comes. Immediate safety is top priority; for now, that's Tas Ralong."

Ellene's smile widened. "Then I offer my assistance in that regard. I can shuttle people on the *Dionysus*, at least thirty at a time."

Finally, she's being helpful. "You'd do that for us?"

"I'm ready to show beyond words what I want to do for your people."

"Alright then."

Selina pulled over a few Regulation officers who set up a transfer with Ellene and the ready-to-move NewEarth refugee population. Soon, a group of residents trudged over toward Ellene's craft. Selina grabbed a few cases of clothing and food to help with the rest of the migration when she caught up with Zed again.

"How's it going?" Zed asked.

"It goes. Although, if anyone asks me when this is gonna end, I may punch 'em."

They shared a laugh. The chronic stress of disruption had washed over the entire NewEarth population. While several of the older generations remembered the first migration to Zormad, the twenty passing cycles mellowed the agitation of uncertainty for those generations and made them more adaptable. However, the severe damage to NewEarth, a civilization that had only begun to expand with new births, was a difficult hurdle for many.

Zed offered the half grin Selina knew meant many things. At that moment, she suspected it was due to her unofficial designation as Ellene chaperone.

"So, how are you and Ellene getting on?"

"Oh, wonderful. She's the perfect mix of inquisitive and annoying I've needed in my life, so thanks for that."

Zed chuckled amid a wince. "Oh, she's not that bad. I guess she mentioned the migration to Yassel."

"Yep."

Zed shrugged with a slight laugh. "Can't say it's the worst idea I've heard. But this quick show of support by the UA after nothing for twenty years has me suspicious."

"Same. So, Zed... you ever gonna tell me why you have me, a Regulation officer for less than a week, spending so much time with her?"

"Simple, she asked for you by name. I was kinda hoping you'd tell me why. Whatever she has in mind for us, you're a big part of it."

Chapter Three

ONCE ELLENE WAS WELL INVOLVED with helping the migration, Selina turned her attention to the breakdown and relocation of the greenhouse facilities and structures. She wasn't as bothered about the physical move as she was about who she had to deal with because of it.

Ryan Rinaldi, lead of the agricultural efforts, was only five years older than Selina. Still, he spoke to her and everyone else as if the entire migration to NewEarth was his idea.

Selina quickly got familiar with Ryan at the NewEarth council meeting right before the Tas Ralong migration started. However, Selina never realized how much anyone in NewEarth hated the Regulation until she heard Ryan's 10-minute barrage of complaints. His detailed and eloquent series of gripes left Selina wondering how Ryan had any time to grow and maintain the crops for NewEarth's food supply.

While Ryan's level of bickering coming from an average citizen would've gotten them dressed down quick, his abilities to produce as many crops as he had gave him a high reputation among NewEarth citizens. A fed dog is loyal to its master, after all, and Ryan's influence over the mood of NewEarth rose commensurate with how well he kept the population fed.

Selina made another pass by the remnants of Ward's Commissary, which by then had dwindled to a shell, with a few more units left to move from it. Ward traded waves with Selina as she walked. Nearby Ward's broken-down site, Selina came across a young couple working on a food development fixture. The man was stooped over the device, holding a section of a food processing unit. He was stocky, with a long mane of curly brownish hair.

"I'll help," Selina said as she trotted over. The agricultural types, known as "Agros," were all devotees to Ryan's groupthink, and this couple was no exception. It was pretty clear to Selina in the deep glare she got from both of them.

Selina grabbed one side of the food device, and the load righted itself as she and the other two walked carefully toward the path to Tas Ralong. After a few moments, Selina said, "We should get this unit onto a landcrawler or the *Dionysus*. It's a long walk to Tas Ralong, ya know."

The man glared. "Sorry, we don't trust the Regulation's landcrawlers with our delicate gear. Ryan wants to supervise all moves once we get to our staging area."

Selina nodded. "Ah. What're your names?"

"Everet." The man answered with the finesse of a boxer's jab.

The woman eyed Selina briefly before saying her name as if it was an alibi. "Claire."

"Well, Everet, Claire... with everyone from NewEarth moving at once, a lot is going on right now. Ryan's probably busy. How about I help you?"

Claire squared her shoulders, taking a step towards Selina with narrowed eyes. Selina bowed her frame in response, inching closer to Claire.

Ward's booming voice interrupted the moment. "What y'all doing, trying to break your backs?"

Ward showed his usual lopsided grin with a curious look in his eyes. Everet cleared his throat. "Nothing you need to worry about."

"Yeah, until I have to cook it up. Why're you walking it? That don't make sense." Ward shook his head, adding a nod to Selina.

Everet took a steady breath and spoke slow and deliberate, with annoyance in his voice. "The system is delicate; I'm worried the jostling might jar something loose."

"And walking it is safer?" Ward shook his head with a chuckle. Selina knew it was up to her. As much as Ryan may have fed his people about not listening to a non-Agro, in the move to Tas Ralong, the Regulation had the rule of law.

"Look, we've moved complex weaponry on these transports. It's not a baby's cradle, but it'll be fine, alright? So again, let's get this loaded. You wouldn't want to be here when the Railen return, right?"

Everet and Claire traded looks, and after a few moments, Everet said, "I'm calling Ryan."

Ward motioned Selina over while Everet and Claire contacted Ryan for a pass by. Selina gazed sharply at Everet, daring him to look up from his comm unit until she felt a nudge from Ward and caught his amused expression.

"Don't be thinking what I think you're thinking over there."

Selina stared at Ward for a second, but his papa-like face melted her resolve, and she chuckled. "Oh, I'd love to teach those two a lesson and good."

Ward snuck his arm around Selina's shoulder. "I know. You've your daddy's temper, no doubt. But since he's not around, I'll have to set you straight."

Selina scoffed. "All they're worried about is their crops and not the odds of being gunned down again out here. Their idealist leader has them believing we can share and be all kumbaya with the rest of Ling Galaxy, but you and I know that ain't so. Like the Railen would be nice if we just fed them, sure."

"I know, Selina. But the truth is we can't survive without Ryan either. No matter what, we've a supply chain, and right now we need Ryan for that."

Selina stared at Ward for a long moment. Survival was a multi-tiered construct. But, the threat to life still hung larger in the balance for her, and the Agros stalling made her nuts.

Selina went ahead and called for a landcrawler vehicle. Several minutes later, with as much pomp as he could've mustered, Ryan showed up. He wore the trademark goggles the Agros used for soil analysis. Ryan first made a big show of looking over the supplies with Everet and Claire without acknowledging the presence of Selina and Ward, who were well within caustic staring distance.

Selina and Ward watched the threesome as they went from reviewing the items on the scene to a pretty spirited talk, with more than a few glances thrown at Selina.

Ward nudged Selina. "Hey, they want me to look at some heavy food prep units. You gonna be okay if I leave you here?"

"I'm fine." She saw the concern with a tinge of doubt in Ward's eyes. "Really, Ward, I'm a big girl."

"No doubt. Still, don't clock anybody. Remember, you're supposed to be keeping the peace."

Selina hugged Ward tightly before he left. The landcrawler arrived a few minutes later. Selina gave the driver the heads up to stand by, and then she headed toward Ryan and the others. Ryan's back was to Selina, but Everet's eyes met hers and he motioned to Ryan, who faced Selina with a look that carried every bit of the smugness Selina expected.

"Ryan, as I told Everet and Claire, we've got the residential side moving. Now, the Agros need to catch up, so we don't disrupt our supply chain more than it already is."

Ryan's mouth formed a line, and he nodded dismissively. "Selina, our equipment is delicate, and that stampede you've got going to Tas Ralong right now doesn't have me too confident in moving our gear just yet."

Selina bristled at Ryan's attitude. In regular times, Selina was ready to cut off someone who wasn't falling in line, but with Ryan, she was far too close to taking a swing at him, but she mustered up one last amount of Regulation reserve for the jerkwad.

"Ryan, I'm sure you saw or heard about that attack by the Railen - you know, the whole reason we're moving in the first place? The Railen aren't gonna care if you've got a few more seedlings to baby or something. If they return and smoke us all, that's gonna be the end of everything, even your little plantings."

Ryan stared at Selina a long moment before he said, "You know, Everet... you and Claire can help me with something back at the greenhouse. So why don't you head over there? I'll finish up here and deal with Selina."

Everet and Claire nodded and walked past, giving Selina another stink eye before leaving the area.

Selina flexed her arms and felt her gut tighten as if she were about to throw a punch. While part of Selina realized Ryan was most likely pushing her buttons, the side of Selina mixed between grieving her mother and stress over protecting those left behind had sapped her patience.

"Ya know, Ryan, all this moving will get people more worked up for food. Ward's operation isn't up yet, so how about we at least get these food crates moving."

Ryan gazed off at the containers. His eyes slid back to Selina, and a smirk found his face. "We'll see. Sure could use a few extra hands with dismantling if you can spare the time, officer."

Selina had ingested a nasty cocktail of equal parts indignation from Ryan and overall fatigue from the NewEarth situation. Having her fill of Ryan for the moment, she said nothing else but instead walked toward the nearby food crates.

Selina grabbed the first container when she felt Ryan's fist slam down hard on her shoulder. "Did I say you could touch *that*?"

Wrong move, guy.

Selina maneuvered Ryan into an armbar and rotated her torso until his body flung over and knocked into another crate. Ryan yelped and gasped as Selina eyed him. "Did I say you could touch *me*? Now then, maybe I didn't make myself clear. I'm taking your food supply to our people. You know, the ones you've been feeding all along? See, they've been moving for a couple of days. A lot haven't eaten much, some not at all. The elderly need extra attention, in case you forgot. Your food production facility is moving in another day. I suggest you make that happen ASAP and don't make me or my team come back here and move it for you because we will, and you won't like how we do it."

"Selina, stop!"

Ward's voice interrupted Selina's thoughts, and she looked at Ward's fearful expression. Then, realizing her overstep, she let Ryan up slowly. Ryan's eyes darted between Ward and Selina, grinning like a lawyer winning a court case. Then, maneuvering his arm around, Ryan said, "Well, let's just see what Zed has to say about this."

Chapter Four

S ELINA AND RYAN'S LITTLE DANCE made the news around NewEarth fast. Even in a mass migration, scrapes between a Regulation officer and the leader of the Agricultural wing were the last thing anyone needed.

Selina regretted losing her cool more than anything she did to Ryan. The jerk had it coming for a while. However, she wasn't looking forward to the collateral damage her tussle did with her standing in Zed's eyes.

Zed and Ryan were already seated in the Regulation temp command center's planning room when Selina arrived. Like the rest of the building, the room was stocked with various supplies.

As bad and annoying as she found it being around Ryan, having Zed mediating made it ten times worse. Selina bristled under Ryan's gaze and contemplated how much popping him good would be worth the extra disciplinary action.

Selina had previously seen Zed agitated during the move, but his anger was directed toward her this time.

"Damn it; we don't have time for this. I'm the lead of NewEarth now, and you both know that. You two will cease whatever's going on here, and you'll do it now, understood?"

Selina swallowed a lump in her throat. "Chief, I was only trying to help them out."

Ryan's eyes avoided Selina's as he leaned forward. "Zed, I appreciate what you've done to keep the peace during this move, but you and your officer here need to know the Agros have the best interests of NewEarth at heart. Given all we've faced, I have to run my program as I've been doing. That includes moving our hardware and crops as I see fit."

Zed stood, and paced around in thought. Selina searched his expression for any hint of what was coming, but came up with nothing. *There's no way he's gonna give Ryan a free pass, is there?*

"Ryan, as far as running your stuff, you're right. But, you have to move faster. Our supplies are stretched along with our people. The more we get to Tas Ralong, the more we'll need the Agros to keep everyone fed. The Regulation will continue to look out for everyone, and you will observe our directions. Even Selina's."

Ryan's lips drew taut, and his eyes darted between Zed and Selina before Ryan offered a slight nod in response.

Zed steepled his fingers. After a few moments, he gave both Selina and Ryan a pointed stare. "OK, we'll get the Agros' food and gear moving quicker, and you two will keep the peace, even if it means being as far the hell away from each other as possible."

An uneasy quiet filled the room after Zed finished. After a few moments, Ryan stood and headed back outside. Selina was about to follow when Zed grabbed her arm.

"Sit down."

A deep ache hit Selina's gut as she slowly pawed for a chair. Zed clasped his hands together in thought.

Oh great, I'm getting a crappy detail as punishment.

"Selina, watch your temper. You're a lot like your old man. He got hot sometimes too."

"Ryan's been pushing me for a while. You know that, right?"

172

"Ryan's a prick, OK? I get it. But he's done a lot for NewEarth, and plenty of people pay attention to what he says. You and I know Ellene's Yassel offer is the best idea. But, the more we're seen lashing out, and the less we keep the peace, the fewer people will listen to whatever we suggest, OK?"

Selina nodded.

"Look, you've been handed a lot real fast. From our first moment in Ling Galaxy, we've never had it easy on NewEarth. Me and your dad Erick used to get in all kinds of problems, fighting off the random raids, bickering with the Mardaks when we were still not on their good side yet. Whenever things got terrible, and I felt like we were a day or two from just being wiped out for good, Erick would look me in the eye and say, 'You never end the fight.' That was him. That kind of determination kept me going then and will keep NewEarth going now."

Hearing stories about her dad that she hadn't heard before was a special kind of salve for Selina. Ever since she lost her father, she pieced together in her mind a quilt work of memories of him. Some were her own recollections, and the rest were stories from Zed.

Zed added, "You're handling a lot pretty damned good, in case you haven't heard that from anyone."

An unexpected burst of emotion hit Selina, and she managed a combination cough and low chuckle at the sudden kudos from her leader. A smile found Selina's lips for the first time in a while. Zed's words and hearing another piece of Erick's history were a welcome boost.

Selina took in a relieved breath and stood. "OK. I'll head back outside, see where else I can help."

Zed smiled back. "By the way, comm just came back about 20 minutes ago. Ellene's finished moving the rest of our group to Tas Ralong. She's coming in and wants to talk more with you."

* * *

As good as Selina felt about standing up to Ryan, she knew Zed was right. Selina hated losing her temper quickly, but nothing had been the same since she returned to Zormad. All the suffering she saw all day long cut her deeply. *The Regulation is supposed to preserve order. But will we ever get back to that order with all that's happened now?*

The *Dionysus* touched down near the makeshift command center with a graceful flourish. After a few minutes, Ellene emerged. Once her eyes met Selina's, Ellene headed over, a smile on her face.

The road ahead for humans had a pretty definite fork in it. On one side stood Tas Ralong, the safe bet. Close by, NewEarth's survivors would be guests of the Mardaks, who at least were marginally interested in having humans around and did not want to blast and pillage them to oblivion. On the other side lay Ellene Ballo and the great unknown of planet Yassel.

Either move was risky, and the time to pick was close.

Selina was about to say hello to Ellene when her comm unit signaled with an alert:

"Omegan unit of starcraft spotted approaching planet Zormad. Alert and activate all available defenses."

Chapter Five

THE SKYLINE TOLD SELINA all she needed. A squadron of Omegan craft flew directly toward the remnants of NewEarth, wings abreast. It was probably another random raid, but any disarrayed group like NewEarth at that point was easy picking for anyone like the Omegans.

As klaxon alarms blared, several Regulation soldiers dashed out of the command center as Ellene looked about.

Ellene's eyes met Selina's, with a glum look. "So, we've got company."

Selina moved her pulse rifle to ready position. "Mmmhmm. I hope the Mardaks are ready for a fight."

The screech of a landcrawler's brakes rang out to Selina's left. Warrah jumped out and ran up close, her curly locks billowed behind her. "What's the plan?"

"Dunno. Zed's getting details and calling for Mardak help in the command center."

Soon, other Regulation landcrawler vehicles arrived at their location. The Mardak militia had maintained a modest force, given all their struggles in Ling overall. Their armory included several light fighters and two medium cruisers. The fleet wasn't tailored for intergalactic conquest, and even a last-stand defense of Zormad was a bit of a stretch. Still, the Mardaks were used to being one of the forgotten races of Ling and had tempered that neglect with a certain stubbornness that kept their race alive.

Ellene grabbed Selina's arm. "I can help."

"Ellene, I'm glad for what you've done so far. But *Dionysus* doesn't look well-armed. I've seen transport ships with more fire-power, frankly."

Ellene laughed. "Oh, Selina, there's more to strength than star-craft weaponry."

Once Zed appeared outside the command center, he was met with a rush of Regulation troops. Selina and Warrah jogged over, arriving as Zed started his briefing. He knelt in the center of the group, glancing about as he spoke.

"The Mardaks will provide help. They're the next biggest target beyond us, and it won't take much for the Omegans to include Tas Ralong in this hit. The problem is they'll need a few minutes, and from the look of those Omegan starcraft, we have a few seconds before we're in the heat."

Warrah scoffed. "We have to hold a spread-out position with maybe two-thirds the force we had before?"

Zed said, "That's right, Warrah. We're 25 strong, but we've gotta fight like 200. So, dig in. The cavalry's coming, but we've got to put as much fire as we can on the Omegans until then. Drivers and gunners, take the landcrawlers, use the pulse cannon. Set up the best perimeter possible. For the rest, find the best fighting positions you can. We'll give them all we got and make them pay for every foot they get closer to us."

The idea of a last stand hadn't occurred to Selina, but the feeling was palpable, and the weary yet resigned glances of her fellow Regulation troops told her that this may be it, and it was time for her to step up with her comrades. Of all NewEarth citizens, the Regulation believed in defense of their lives with force. Their job wasn't determining the political nuances of the topsy turvy world of Zormad or Ling Galaxy. They just knew a job was there to be done, and that job at times involved force. It was in their hearts to protect what was left of NewEarth to the last person, weapon, and round.

The troops gave a rousing shout before heading to the fight. Selina's heart thumped in her throat, realizing their odds against the Omegans couldn't have been worse if they all lay flat on the sand, their arms raised in surrender. Still, she pushed forward, heading toward the landcrawler with Warrah, when she felt a hand on her shoulder and turned to Ellene.

As several Regulation troops nearby began digging in, Selina suddenly realized she was stuck in place. Her feet felt like they were tied to the Zormad surface, and her attempts to move only hurt her legs.

What is this? Am I panicking?

Warrah yelled for Selina to take cover, but Selina remained stationary. Then, Ellene's gaze finally told Selina her body wasn't frozen from panic but something Ellene had done herself.

"Ellene, we've got this." Selina's tone had every bit of the emphasis of an order behind it, even though she was still frozen in place.

Ellene's warm eyes darkened suddenly, so much it made Selina nervous. When Ellene spoke again, her vocal pattern twisted with an ethereal sound. "Selina, you don't want to do this."

Something in either the change in Ellene's eyes or maybe her vocal inflection jarred Selina. She held her weapon up and slightly pointed away from Ellene. "Excuse me?"

Ellene smirked amid narrowed eyes. Her glance darted toward an Omegan craft that darted past them. "I said you don't want to do this."

Selina felt fear in her gut as Warrah took off in the landcrawler. "Ellene, what's going on?"

"Selina, I'm sorry. I haven't told you everything yet. I wanted you to make your own decision about what you and your people do, but to do that, I first need to show you just why I'm so interested in you."

Selina knew fairy tales. Those stories were one of the carryovers from Earth that remained with their new civilization on Zormad. But, for most of her adult life to that point, she assumed stories about wizards and brave warriors on journeys fighting evil creatures and mythical spirits were an invention of desperate parents attempting to give their children something to cling to, something to focus on, but mostly to get them to sleep.

But what Ellene did next was like nothing Selina had ever heard about in any story or real account.

Ellene strode toward the Omegan craft, which swooped down and fired indiscriminately at the rubble of NewEarth, the ground, and in some cases, running individuals. The sky had darkened with smoke, and the bevy of Omegan starcraft circled overhead like a pack of hungry predators savoring the scent of the kills, both the fresh ones and the ones about to happen.

Explosions from rocket fire punched the air. The foul stench of burning pieces of fabricated building components itched Selina's nose.

Ellene walked through the fray with studied calm. Selina yelled for Ellene to take cover, but Ellene never acknowledged Selina. Ellene instead climbed on a pile of rubble, formerly a piece of housing, and flung off her cape. The overhead craft slowed their pace as a deep rumbling sound built.

Ellene stood and glanced about. Her long mane of blonde hair wisped about like sprigs of wheat in a gentle breeze. Her light bluish skin stood out sharply against the gray background.

Ellene's slender body arched into a fighting stance, and a screech pierced the air. Selina grabbed her ears and noticed several others nearby did the same; their faces strained with the overwhelming noise. Selina looked about for the noise source but realized it was Ellene, whose flowing golden locks of hair had burst into flames. Selina caught a glimpse of Ellene's face when she looked back, and Selina gasped at the sight.

Ellene's eyes became two glowing orbs which cast bright yellow light as intense as a sun. Suddenly, a sizeable Omegan starcraft bore down on her. Ellene thrust her arms up toward the approaching ship, and a series of energy bolts burst from her hands toward the craft, shattering it into a spectacular explosion. Barrage after barrage of pulse cannon fire from other Omegan ships hammered the ground around Ellene, but she stayed in place, casting out more energy bolts that sliced any craft that flew too close to them. The sky lit up with explosions.

Then, Ellene flung herself up into the air and flew on an attack through the rest of the pursuing Omegan barrage until finally, the remaining ships turned in retreat.

Once the threat was gone, Ellene lowered herself back to the ground. The air was filled with the stench of smoke. Wails from the injured drifted over the air along with the wafts of smog. Selina, realizing she was still holding her ears, slowly lowered her hands and walked toward Ellene.

Ellene picked up her cape and adjusted her hair as if she hadn't just self-levitated and vaporized a group of Omegan starcraft with beams from her own body.

Ellene hadn't acknowledged Selina, instead she glanced around, her eyes showing sadness when she saw the hurt Mardaks and humans.

Selina remembered all the fights she and the Regulation had been in, especially the last showdown with the Railen. *Ellene could've headed off all of those attacks by herself.* Selina saw Zed, and he had a look on his face that Selina imagined matched hers.

"What the hell was that, Ellene?"

Ellene simply gazed coolly back at Selina, then Zed for a moment. Her expression then warmed a bit, and she managed a polite smile. "Essence, Selina. That's why I need your help so badly."

Selina blinked. "*My* help?"

Ellene smiled. "We'll talk about that very soon."

Moving to Yassel was still a risk and a long shot for safety. But, having Ellene's power as security would've made the trip much safer. Selina only wondered about her part in Ellene's strange powers.

Zed cleared his throat. "Well, that was... great and scary at the same time. Do you mind telling us why you didn't bust that out sooner?"

Ellene's smile was a mix of triumph and concern. Ellene approached Selina and Zed as the landcrawler vehicles nearby came in closer to their spot. "I don't like to direct through fear. That's Malone Stanton's way. However, powers like mine are terrifying to the uninitiated, and I intend to use reason to convince you to come to planet Yassel. I would greatly appreciate if you let me explain this to everyone."

Zed replied, "OK, Ellene. It's still everyone's choice whether they stay or go, of course."

Whether or not they went to Yassel, Ellene's performance wasn't going to be secret very long around NewEarth. Selina only wondered if it was enough to convince those who rooted themselves in the idea of gathering and hunkering like Ryan and his posse of Agros.

Chapter Six

THE TAS RALONG WAREHOUSE THAT became NewEarth's new location was a vast structure. A collection of several medium-sized buildings connected via corridors and featuring a large common area, the once cold and stark facility took on new life as a hasty collection of living areas. A makeshift platform stage was built toward the front entrance using a series of emptied storage crates.

Once a bulk of NewEarth residents gathered in the common area, they were ready for Ellene's presentation. Selina stood at the side of the stage with Zed and Ellene at center. Dirty faces in the crowd were a standard dress. Selina imagined she looked pretty messed up herself, given all the moving and dragging of equipment she did in the dry Zormad heat and dust.

Another common trait in their group was fatigue. The fear of being killed by the Railen was terrible enough, but a forced evacuation of everything they owned in days with little to no sleep had everyone looking wearier than they had ever been.

The warehouse's interior boomed with the crowd's sound, but

Zed quieted them down after a few moments. "OK, everyone, we've all been through a lot, and despite that, I'm glad to see we've gotten this move done pretty well. Ellene Ballo of Grondia wants to talk with us. She recently helped turned back an Omegan raid on our group, so for me that earns her a few minutes of our time to hear what she's got to say."

Selina searched faces in the crowd. Many looked at least curious about Ellene. She also saw the Agros, Ryan smack in their middle, the lot of them toward the crowd's right.

"Citizens of NewEarth, my name is Ellene Ballo of the Nara. Your time in Ling Galaxy has been fraught with danger, struggle at best. I'm here today to offer you a chance to rise above that. You may have heard of our race. First, let me say we've been stewards of Ling Galaxy and Essence for millennia.

"I want you to know we're aware of your history in this galaxy so far. You've been mistreated, and while we haven't been able to help you in the past, we've taken steps. Unfortunately, Ling Galaxy has plummeted into war. Malone Stanton and the Omegans are making their play for control of Ling and the Nara. That means things will only get worse for everyone, including you here. But I want you to know there are many fighting for peace. The Universal Alliance stands as a beacon for order, and as a full supporter of the UA, I'm here to say you've got an option beyond your current agreement."

Shouts from the crowd interrupted Ellene. Not a surprise, the other Agros nearby had adopted Ryan's outrage.

Ellene continued in her speech. "The truth is, you are not safe here. It would be best if you came with me to planet Yassel, the seat of the UA. I understand the risks are considerable. But I ask you to think of the risk of doing nothing. You've already lost your temporary home, and that was to a smaller group of Railen. The Omegans have also shown themselves very recently, and Malone Stanton remains a huge threat. How long do you think you'll last hunkered down on a Far Reach planet before another attack? Spirits preserve you if the Railen or Omegans determine this entire planet as a strategic target."

Ryan's shouts got much clearer. "We've survived for over twenty years now. If any are to blame for our problems, it's the Regulation, agitating outsiders like the Railen. I say these attacks are their fault."

Shouts came in response to Ryan, mainly from his fellow Agros propping up their fearless leader. Worse, Selina saw others in the crowd who weren't Argos but still clapped in approval of Ryan's theory.

Ellene's eyes met Selina's. Wordlessly, Selina saw something in Ellene's gaze that said *no one believes that. Trust me, what this man says will only harm your people if he convinces others. Stick with me, and we'll sway them.*

Selina took a sharp breath in and held it. She balled her hands into fists so tight they burned.

Turning back to the crowd, Ryan in particular, Ellene continued, "I know much of what you've suffered hasn't been anything in your control."

Ryan sneered. "Maybe Malone isn't so bad after all. From what I've heard on Network, it sounds like Malone's got the right idea of caring for everyone. For that matter, maybe Essence itself is where we should focus. I heard it revitalized a whole planet. So why shouldn't we look for Malone's help, and not yours?"

Ellene's face changed immediately with Ryan's challenge. She walked off the stage and into the crowd, until she stood face to face with Ryan. Selina looked at Zed, who shrugged.

Ellene stretched her arms out so her robe billowed and straightened over her frame. Her tone became gentler than Selina would've expected. "I understand your distrust, Xeno. However, you must realize Ling Galaxy is filled with many races of beings, and most had suffered long before you arrived. My kind has fueled this galaxy, but with that comes a delicate balance to maintain. Don't you think we would've used our control over Essence to destroy Malone and the rest if we had the ability? We need all races working together to handle the needs of the many. Safety and security only happen through cooperation. Essence doesn't offer perfection; it only offers life."

Ellene glanced about before facing Ryan again, her eyes staring like a medium deeply into Ryan's nonplussed expression. "You and everyone else must hear my next words and remember them well, or it could mean the end for all of us. Malone Stanton is not your savior. He's not the one to bring anything to Ling Galaxy other than his special variety of chaos."

Ellene pointed a finger toward Ryan. "This one might tell you about Malone Stanton's miracle on the Agmon planet. Agmon, a near lifeless body not unlike Zormad, was returned to a lush paradise teeming with life and sustenance thanks to Malone's wielding of Essence. But, be warned, those manipulations have caused imbalances in Essence that have already begun to degrade life elsewhere in Ling Galaxy.

"Malone is quite clever and has gotten a special order of followers in short time. He promises things like saving worlds and letting all Essence flow freely. But, Essence was never meant to be molded by any living being, served to do the will of one. Malone wants everyone to believe he can provide life to all and hold everyone hostage to his plans, but his desires only lead to destruction. Essence flows from Grondia, and that creation lets Ling Galaxy exist. That creation exists through a careful balance of energy, which the Nara oversee. If Essence is overused, it could destroy the galaxy. That's a very inconvenient fact for the likes of Malone to mention, but one you should all be very concerned about."

Selina saw the crowd flare up into a series of conversations and heated arguments. She edged closer to Zed and nudged him. "What do you think of all this?"

Zed folded his arms as they both studied the crowd below. "Ellene wouldn't have bothered with us if we weren't useful to her somehow. In any case, there won't be any quality of life on Zormad for us. Of course, people like the easy path, which for now is staying.

Maybe this convinces enough of them about going to Yassel. That may be the best thing we've done in Ling Galaxy yet."

Selina agreed on the move, but her role regarding Essence left her wondering just what this migration to Yassel would cost her in the end.

Chapter Seven

ELLENE'S OFFER TO NEWEARTH went as well as Selina could've predicted. Out of 3000 people, 1700 agreed to the trip to Yassel. What remained after the vote was the dividing of essentials and preparing for departure.

The NewEarth council gathered in the admin room of the warehouse to review the next step in the transport to planet Yassel. The growing pomp of their body was quickly reduced to partially slipshod chairs huddled around a rusted-out table.

Zed began, "The transport the UA is sending, *Evangeline*, has enough space if anyone changes their minds about coming along. I know this is sudden; believe me, I wish there was more time to investigate alternatives."

Selina caught Ryan's cocky grin. In the division among those leaving and staying, Ryan was elevated to leader of NewEarth. Selina couldn't have been leaving the colony soon enough after that.

"Something on your mind there, Ryan?" Asked Zed.

Ryan cast an annoyed look at Zed and Selina as he stood. "A few things. We've busted our asses developing sustenance for NewEarth, not to mention getting on the good graces of - I don't know - the only group of aliens in this galaxy so far who haven't minded us breathing their air. Now, we're being penalized into giving up crops because some of us naively think the UA will save us?"

Selina grasped the handle of her pulse pistol and squeezed it tight.

Ryan continued his sermon. "Sorry, I don't see why we should jump on board with the UA just because they claim their location is more secure. Besides, isn't planet Yassel under attack by the Omegans now? I know that's true, even with the spotty connection to Network that we have."

Selina said, "Safer is better than nothing. Excuse me if I don't trust this building that was probably here way before we set foot on this planet. You wanna stay, bone up on your Mardak and blend into Tas Ralong? That's on you. But you've got a week to make up your mind."

Ryan narrowed his eyes. "I'll have you all know I'm telling anyone that'll listen why they should stay too, including those who voted for a ride on your little transport. So have fun with your new captors."

Ryan slid his chair back, making a loud screech. Zed reached for him as he left, but it was useless. "Selina, get a head count of people and let's start organizing. I don't want to hold this over any more than we have to. It's a helluva long way to Yassel."

Chapter Eight

EVANGELINE LANDED ON ZORMAD a few days past the estimated arrival date. After a lengthy approach sequence, the transport eased to a gentle touchdown a hundred yards from the outskirts of Tas Ralong. The craft, a large oblong sphere, was decorated with an array of lights cascading in sequence about the fuselage. A progressive chain of living quarters and common areas adorned the ship from aft to fore. A massive bank of engines at the rear gave off an intense hum as they cycled during the ship's landing phase.

Selina worked with the Regulation and ran shuttles to and from the craft loading food stores and other supplies. Like the earlier migration, a new procession formed of those loading themselves and spare items aboard for the trip to planet Yassel.

While helping with the loading process, Selina noticed a change in the general expressions of her fellow humans from earlier. Where the looks of fatigue and worry were familiar after the Railen assault, and even in the temporary warehouse, now there were many more looks of hope. Those who committed to the Yassel move showed the relief pretty clearly on their faces without needing any verbal response.

Ellene stood next to Selina, a hopeful smile on her face. "Well, what do you think?"

Selina felt herself smile as she answered. "I have to say, I'm impressed. We're not used to others helping us except for the Mardaks."

Ellene nodded. "I hope you realize now I hold you and your kind's safety as a priority."

"Mmmhmm."

"I understand some refused to join us?"

Selina glanced offward and nodded quickly. "Some still don't trust the UA."

"And you do?" Ellene pawed Selina's shoulder

Selina's face flushed hot. She freed herself of Ellene's grasp. "I trust you to deliver, and you've done that so far."

Three UA fighters stood alongside the *Evangeline*. The sleek black starcraft consisted of a slender central tube with a pair of swept backward wings, each featuring a barrage of missiles and pulse cannon. Toward the rear, two tail fins angled upward and out. *Well, their fighters look tough enough. I just hope their flyers they got for this have the chops for handling trouble.*

The UA fighter pilots' all-black suits gave off a surprising gleam in the muted sunshine of the overcast and windblown air on Zormad.

"Shouldn't we have more of an escort?" Selina asked Ellene.

Ellene shrugged. "I've seen fighter compliments of three before. Don't forget, *Dionysus* will be along too. It's not as agile as those fighters, but we'll have some protection on our journey."

Selina went to leave, but Ellene held her close. "I promised we'd talk about Essence and what I have in mind for you, so let's do that on our voyage."

* * *

189

The scene of the NewEarth residents boarding *Evangeline* was a tapestry of emotion. The crowd of departing citizens and remaining residents milled about outside the ark ship. Between teary goodbyes between the departing and those staying behind and frantic arguments over what possessions were necessary, the story of NewEarth's life had taken an unexpected turn toward a marked division.

Selina wondered if she'd ever see those staying behind on Zormad again. Despite all the problems of Zormad, it gave humans a home in Ling Galaxy. Selina hoped the opportunities were greater in the world of Yassel, with more of a thriving metropolis.

With the loading of *Evangeline* almost complete, and the boarding of her passengers underway, Selina strolled through the crowds and back into Tas Ralong for one last bit of unfinished business.

Zed was clear in his order, but Selina wasn't ready to let things go with Ryan. *If I can get the creep to go to Yassel, we'll save more people along the way when his devotees see their big guy isn't so against the move after all.*

Selina found Ryan working on the last group of crops to be delivered to *Evangeline*. Ryan handled the delicate vegetation as if it were a newborn child. For all purposes, it may well have been. Crops weren't limitless, and Ryan's food was sure going to be a significant part of their survival until their place on Yassel was established.

Ryan spoke without glancing up at Selina.

"Are you here to help me move these seedlings?"

Selina walked about while Ryan continued working on the garden trough with a gleeful smile. He had secured a lot of food for sure. Several crates stood by, ready for relocation.

"Ryan, I don't wanna hear you bitching about how I'm doing it wrong. So, how's about that?"

"Then what *are* you here for, Selina?"

"Giving you one last chance to see if you'd change your mind, come along to Yassel and keep our people together."

Ryan's eyes met Selina's. After a defiant laugh, he shook his head. "Oh, you just can't take it, can you?"

"Take what?"

"The possibility someone else has a better idea than your trip to Yassel. I hope you have some protection - some pulse weapons at least. You're about to be outnumbered, and I hope you didn't just sign yourselves up to be some experiment for the UA."

While Selina's muscles ached, she held herself in check. *The fool isn't worth it.* "We're almost completely loaded; make sure your supplies get on board."

"Will do," Ryan muttered.

"Good luck in the wild," Selina said, her arms folded.

Ryan's eyes narrowed and a smirk found his lips. "That's more than I'd expect from you or anyone else from the Regulation."

"That's all you're gonna get. You really doing this, huh?"

For the first time, Selina caught a sincere glimmer behind Ryan's eyes as he studied her for a moment. "I know you don't understand my choice. I don't trust well-meaners like Ellene. I've listened to Network, just like you. You think you're getting some lavish life up there on Yassel? I'll be surprised if you even get there without being picked off by a squadron of Omegans in a few days."

Selina knew Ryan's bleak outlook wasn't totally out of the possibilities for them. But she'd been into the Tas Ralong scene, and what she'd heard of the rest of Zormad hadn't offered any more promise.

"Ya know, Ryan, you've been a big pain in the ass for a while now. Just because the Regulation has some presence and can defend our people, it doesn't mean we brought those attacks on ourselves."

Ryan chuckled again, then strode around his greenery, his pride and joy, as if the vegetation was an expanded audience on his side that cast jeers and insults Selina's way. He finally flung his arms over-head. "Life is about more than taking aim, Selina. What we give back to people matters more. Maybe one day you'll learn that. I'm sorry you lost your father and now your mother, I am. My folks made it a few years after I was born; they're both gone now too. Fact is, we're in

Ling Galaxy now, and the best thing we can do is keep out of the way of this fight Ellene mentioned. Yeah, I saw what she did against the Omegans. We're ants to them, Selina. I'd rather settle for a quiet place out of the fray. That's my way. You do yours."

Selina knew she just got as much closure as she would ever have from Ryan. There was no winning him over, and she was OK with that, but the lingering contempt for the protection NewEarth had been under was a bitter taste she knew she wouldn't wash out of her mouth anytime soon. "You better reach out to the Mardaks. They're your best shot for support now if things get rough again."

Ryan nodded, not looking up.

"Goodbye, Ryan. Take care of what's left of NewEarth for us." Selina started walking away until Ryan's voice stopped her.

"Wait."

Unlike before, Selina noticed that Ryan's shields of arrogance and self-righteousness weren't there, and his tone sounded more like a concerned family member.

"Take care of yourself too, Selina."

Chapter Nine

EVANGELINE SHUDDERED AS ITS thrusters built
strength to lift the mammoth starcraft off the ground. Soon
it eased through the air, slow and gently. Joined by the UA
fighters and the *Dionysus*, the convoy quickly shot to the skies,
leaving Zormad behind.

While the interior of *Evangeline* was cleaner than the filthy
Zormad warehouse, the temperature aboard was much more relaxed
than the radiant heat to which humans had acclimated on Zormad.
The corridors of the *Evangeline* were bright, with blue and white
luminescent accents woven into a pattern on the walls. Selina was
impressed with the UA's attention to detail on an Ark ship. While
she'd only seen remnants of *Intrepid*, the craft used in the initial trek
to NewEarth, that ship was far less elaborate than *Evangeline*.

One primary access corridor ran through the center of *Evangeline*, like a spinal column. Connecting side pathways several hundred
feet from each other lead to the individual sleeping quarters. Selina
strolled around the hallways as the craft shuddered and rumbled on
its way. She spent a few minutes walking around, checking how the

NewEarthers were settling in for the trip. Soon, Selina came across Warrah, reviewing a hand terminal.

"Look at you, embracing the UA tech early."

Warrah glanced up, her long curly hair wisped to one side. "I'm not letting anyone get one up on us. The more we know about Yassel and these people before we get there, the better off we'll be."

"So, what are you learning then?"

"So far, I'm pulling details about *Evangeline*. The ship can do basic but not transient warp."

"Anything else good, like rooms bigger than ten feet square?" Selina chuckled.

"Nothing worth mentioning so far."

Selina ran a finger along the terminal, which displayed a wire-frame model of the ark ship. She flung her finger about, and the display updated to show the locations of the residents on board.

Warrah shrugged. "We have enough rations to hold us for a month. Since they sent *Evangeline* to us, I'm hoping they'll help if we need something, but we'll see, right?"

Selina smiled at her friend. "I'm glad you're here. This would've sucked without you."

"By the way, Ket's a jerk, OK?"

A lock of hair fell across one of Warrah's eyes, but her supportive smile wasn't covered by anything. The pangs Selina felt since she parted with Ket remained. "I know. I'll be fine; I will."

"I mean, if you ask me - and you still haven't but should've, I think you should've clocked the dude. He sees NewEarth on fire, people running for cover, and he doesn't offer to help?"

"He's a fortune chaser, Warrah. At least we didn't have him along to see him bail when things got rough."

"True that." Warrah gave Selina a side hug. "Besides, you still got me - I can't leave my training sister behind, now can I?"

Selina leaned forward until their heads touched. "Well, sister, I gotta head back to my room. I'm due for a little chat with Ellene on things."

* * *

Selina had many worries about what close exposure to Essence could mean for her. She'd heard stories about people physically harmed or even obliterated through the power of Essence. The display Ellene put on during the NewEarth attack was a pretty clear example of how destructive the stuff could be.

Selina activated the comm portal in her room, and Ellene's face appeared on screen after a few moments.

"How are your new accommodations?"

Selina looked at her spartan quarters. If it weren't for the somewhat adequate bedding, hygiene station, and comm setup, she'd have easily compared it with a holding cell at the Regulation precinct. "OK, I guess. We won't be here forever, so that makes it tolerable."

"I know. So, to start, let me take you back to the early times of Ling Galaxy."

Ellene's eyes darted about; her mouth drew into a line. The existence of the galaxy through Essence was probably not going to be handled in a single conversation. "Ling Galaxy came to be through a series of cosmic shifts over hundreds of millennia ago, where the earliest forms of Essence generated an entire galaxy around itself. Planets, moons, stars, and everything else came into being over many cycles, what your kind knows as years. Among these celestial bodies, Grondia was formed near the center of Ling, as the wellspring from which Essence emanates."

"So, Essence... is it an energy source?"

"In Essence's most common state, it provides for life and sustenance on an entire planet. The Nara were the first life forms in Ling Galaxy, and we were taught about Essence."

"Taught by who?" Selina asked.

"They are known to us as the Gazer. An ethereal form that gave existence to all life in Ling Galaxy and created Essence, which flows from Grondia. The Nara were charged with being stewards of the Essence in service of the Gazer.

"From there, life began in Ling Galaxy and grew over thousands of cycles. Other planets were formed and populated. Civilizations developed, and the Nara kept their word as first in Ling to bring Essence out to all worlds, sustaining them and life in the galaxy.

"With that life came freedom for all, which eventually caused other things to happen. But, as you know, life doesn't always follow a straight path. Eventually, imbalances appeared. At first, it was greed for more resources. Then, others wanted more control, selfish thinking infected the minds of many, and fighting ensued. Finally, the Nara themselves were challenged to maintain their mission. So, the Scions were created."

"The Scions?"

"Imbued with the very Essence itself and given abilities, like what I did back on Zormad. A Scion's task was to maintain order, and keep the balance in Ling."

"What do you mean by balance?"

"The life Essence creates and makes possible only happens when the flow of Essence guided by the Nara is properly maintained. We simply call this the balance. But, even with Essence in its normal state, suffering still remained. Those ills come from the freedom of choice all in Ling Galaxy have. Some choose greed, corruption, and actions like those lead to wars like the one we are currently experiencing."

"But, you had Scions. Why didn't you set up every Nara as a Scion up to keep control?"

"We tried that, with several volunteers. That painful process taught us of the strong temptation with Essence. It can tempt even the noblest Nara, and pull at the tiniest of the mind's imperfections. A mind not as focused and pure can be swayed, and the power Essence offers can become a tool for the wrong individual. Even the Nara, raised in isolation from the galaxy, aren't immune to that lure of power. Malone Stanton is a prime example. He was once every bit the Nara citizen I am. Had we given him this power, Ling Galaxy may not have lasted until now."

Selina shuddered. "Well, I don't know where you got the idea about us, but we're not near perfect either."

"I know, Selina. It's an enormous risk that could have serious consequences for you. That said, the war upon this galaxy makes some risks worth considering. Your kind has shown enough resilience through the long trip you made here. That shows you've got a rugged spirit."

"But is that enough?"

"I'm willing to bet it is, Selina. Ling Galaxy has always had freedom, but safety is a challenge. Having justice will keep us safe, and I think the Scions are what we need for that to happen."

Selina's thoughts went to Kreela, the kindly old Mardak woman who latched onto Selina so abruptly when the two met at the trading market on Zormad.

"Ellene, not long ago, I met a Mardak female named Kreela who was very interested in me. She kept talking about how I had something going on, something I wasn't aware of yet. Is that why you're so fascinated by me? Are you seeing something in me like this Kreela did?"

Ellene nodded slowly. "There is a prophecy from ancient Nara times called the One from Without. It talks about a period of terrible tribulation in Ling Galaxy, where the very fabric of existence will be nearly torn by someone called the Great Usurper. Through the power of diplomacy, this Usurper rallies a large army to their side and wages war against the very heart of Ling Galaxy. Many die as a result of this, but in time, the One from Without rises up to destroy the Usurper and restores peace to Ling Galaxy."

An empty feeling welled in the pit of Selina's stomach. Ellene's original request quickly went from simple to gargantuan. "Ellene, what exactly are you seeing in me? I'd like to know. Frankly, I'm not feeling like much of a hero at all right now. I couldn't save my people from getting killed by the Railen or Omegans, and I've been stumbling to figure things out ever since."

Selina buried her face in her hands as her body shook with sobs.

The emotions poured out of her; at least she was alone, not around the UA or other Regulation officers.

Ellene's voice softened. "Selina, look at me."

Through a veil of tears, Selina gazed into Ellene's warm face.

"I'm going to be there with you, and I won't lead you astray. Remember, everyone has a place, and you matter."

Selina climbed onto her bed, wishing she could've asked her mother for her thoughts on her predicament, at the very least to have a hug.

* * *

With several weeks remaining before their arrival on Yassel, Selina's routine for the voyage slowly took shape. Talks with Ellene about the Scions and Essence, regular rounds of the ship, and the occasional pissing contest with the UA troops aboard who were more than determined to assert their control.

Selina was on one of her regular strolls when rhythmic footsteps sounded behind her. Two UA Sentries approached from up the hall. It was the humans' ride, but it was still the UA's craft. The duo of officers stopped when they neared Selina and gave a polite nod.

The two guards were humanoid in appearance, but they gave Selina the same vibe she'd gotten since humans set foot on the craft. This voyage wasn't a benevolent rescue. It was more like the UA was checking off a list.

The stockier sentry spoke first. "Something wrong, Xeno?" Their uniform showed UA Officer insignia on the collar.

"I'm checking on our people. Habit from being a peacekeeper on Zormad."

Officer Stocky's vocal patterns loudened into a bark. "That's unnecessary. Security is covered. Better get back to your room. Never know when we'll hit a rough spot on this trip."

"Rough spot?"

The other UA sentry spoke with a nasal tone. "Asteroids, debris?"

The tone of the duo's answers was way more coddling than Selina wanted, needed, or was up for tolerating. "You know, we have our peacekeeping force, which is UA affiliated. Maybe you haven't heard of the Regulation, but we kept the peace on a Far Reach planet for over twenty years before you all showed up."

Stocky's mouth drew into a line. "That's fine, but we've orders to keep this voyage on track, and we don't want disruptions."

So, we're a disruption now? "Mmmhmm." Selina's jaw twitched. Clearly, they weren't interested, but Selina figured she'd find the group's commanding officer and see if maybe the UA goodwill hadn't flowed down from the top yet.

"OK then. If you boys need any assistance yourselves, let me know."

The two eyed each other for a moment. Then, finally, the stocky one glanced back at Selina slightly amusedly. "We'll be fine."

Without any other acknowledgment, the sentries continued down the hall. Selina felt a slight sting at the brush aside but kept on her original path. She'd been through enough, and even a UA Sentry wasn't going to brush her aside that easy.

Selina wandered up to the *Evangeline* fore section and found Captain Farlane studying charts of the remainder of the journey to Yassel. Farlane eyed Selina with an annoying glare, his mouth in a firm line.

Still ticked at her run in with the UA sentries, Selina scoffed and leaned back against the wall, her arms folded, giving Farlane her best burning scowl.

Several chirping alerts from a nearby console distracted Farlane. Once he tapped a few controls, he looked back at Selina. "What's wrong?"

"First of all, you should've told your crew this babysitting they're doing isn't necessary. We're not terrorists. We're scared people trying to get to safety. Second, how about telling us more about what's ahead for us on Yassel? All we know so far is Ellene Ballo wants us there.

I'm not getting a warm and fuzzy that anyone else on this ship cares, including you, Captain."

Farlane closed up the charts and held them across his chest. Selina noticed a bit of recognition on his face as he stood, his head downward in thought. After a minute, their eyes met again. "I don't know the plans for your people because no one has told me anything. We were ordered to bring you to planet Yassel, and this was given top priority. But, since you're pretty observant, I'll add that several parties don't think this operation was in the best interests of the UA in general."

Selina narrowed her eyes.

Farlane continued, "Ellene Ballo has enough influence to override many objections, making this trip possible."

"Then what do you think, Captain?" Selina added weight to the last word, spoken like it was more accusation than recognition. "I have to say the UA guard patrols give me a strong prison vibe. According to Ellene Ballo, we're a little treasure. Whatever we end up being worth, for all we've been through, we deserve more dignity than this."

Farlane wrinkled his nose. "You think you're the only ones who've had it bad in Ling Galaxy? Let me tell you something; we had problems long before your kind showed up. Malone, the Omegans, and Railen are the latest troublemakers around here. The UA's been cleaning up messes since before you were born, and things aren't settling anytime soon. So, sit back, and be grateful someone decided to give a damn about you. There's plenty who'd kill for what you've been given."

Selina leaned back against the bulkhead, the confusion in her deepening. *If this was the welcome wagon, what's waiting for us at Yassel? Maybe this trip was a mistake?*

Farlane continued, "I'm no diplomat, and I disagree on sending a large transport with minimal starcraft escort into open UA space in the middle of a war." Farlane's lips drew taut. "When you're in a position like mine, you get used to giving and dealing with the hard truth, and that's what it is."

"Uh-huh. Well, sorry to spoil whatever you had planned, but there's almost two thousand people on this craft with no say in what's happened to them since we've been in Ling Galaxy. I know there's a war on, but how about some damn respect for Ellene Ballo and what she sees in us that you haven't considered?"

Farlane's gaze held on Selina. She folded her arms, her breaths came quick and short, but she stayed still. They both remained like that until more warnings sounded on the console. "Ugh, proximity indicators again. Look, I don't have to like my orders to follow them, OK? Now excuse me, navigating through rogue asteroid belts isn't exactly an autopilot procedure."

After Selina left the bridge, she made one more pass through the halls, with an extra effort to walk close to the passing UA guards, before returning to her room. She almost entered when she saw Warrah approaching slowly.

"You OK, Selina? I heard your chat with Farlane."

"Oh yeah, how?"

"I was at a console seeing what info on Yassel I could pull on a scan."

"Uh huh. I'm fine. I just..." Selina thrust herself back against the bulkhead near her door. As she looked into Warrah's concerned eyes, thoughts raced in Selina's mind: about what she'd seen since being on board, Ellene's words to her, and how important she and the rest were supposed to be. It was a mismatch, and Selina was ready for the truth to come out, whatever that was.

Chapter Ten

BLARING KLAXON ALARMS GOT the next word in between Selina and Warrah. After a few moments, a group of six UA soldiers with pulse weapons jogged past, grim looks on their faces.

"Wonder what that's about?" Warrah asked.

"Whatever it is, I don't think it's a drill."

A series of loud blasts sounded in the distance, and the floor beneath them shook.

"Are we... under attack?" Selina asked.

"OK, I'm gonna find Zed. Meet me in the supply room."

After Warrah took off down the hall, Selina had another thought. She slipped back into her room, and opened the comm back to Ellene. The video screen remained blank at first, but then Ellene appeared. The fear on her face was unmistakable.

"Ellene, what's going on? We hear blasts outside the ship-"

"-the Omegans have engaged us. Selina, I don't have time to tell you more; just please listen. If the Omegans capture you, just follow along."

"Follow along?!? I thought we were fighting them!"

"There's more to it. Look, we'll send someone, I pro-"

The line went blank.

Panic hit Selina like a slap to her face. *Was Ellene killed? No, that couldn't have happened. Why does she want us to follow along if the Omegans capture us?*

A series of shouts came from the hall outside her door, along with quick footsteps in both directions. Whatever was happening, she had a job to do. That preceded any grand plans Ellene had and any One from Without junk.

The Regulation and whatever UA Unit is here will defend this place to the last. Maybe there's hope for the calvary yet? Selina grabbed her contact token for the *Crimson Lance*. Ket was probably too far away to make it in time for anything. Even if he did, what could he do against the Omegan squadron out there? Still, it was worth a shot.

Selina placed the token in her comm portal and sent a simple message to Ket.

KET, WE'RE IN TROUBLE. ARK SHIP *EVANGELINE* UNDER ATTACK FROM OMEGANS EN ROUTE TO PLANET YASSEL!

Chapter Eleven

SELINA TROTTED UP TOWARD THE FRONT of the ship. Farlane wasn't around, so she grabbed another of the crew.

"What's going on?"

The officer's face twisted in agitation. "What are you doing here?"

Selina's face flushed hot. "Stop treating us like cargo and tell me what the hell's out there!"

The officer narrowed his eyes. "Alright, an Omegan Horde unit looking for trouble found us."

Selina knew about the Omegan Horde. The Omegans kept a significant presence throughout Ling Galaxy, and the word about their horde was even if the unit seen was small, others were likely not far away. The smart move was never threatening a horde unit because your odds could quickly turn sour. This threat, even when only perceived, gave the Omegans more confidence to agitate and lash out at will around Ling Galaxy.

Selina saw six starcraft on a nearby monitor, one of which was a large cruiser. In addition, one of the UA fighters escorting the *Evangeline* exploded from a missile blast.

"What about the *Dionysus*?"

The officer barked several orders into the comm before he gave Selina a why-are-you-still-here look.

"The *Dionysus* took heavy fire, best we can tell, they escaped."

Escaped? Ellene handled Omegan starcraft when she was by herself, why couldn't she do more in a ship?

"You gonna call for backup?" Selina asked.

"Just stay out of the way and get back to your bunk." The officer returned to a monitor console, looking at damage indicators for *Evangeline.*

Screw this. Selina bolted back into the main hallway, past a group of UA soldiers racing toward the bridge, and headed for the storage area for NewEarth.

The interior lighting on *Evangeline* dimmed. Several people ran back and forth, and the hall was filled with shouts from several directions. Selina felt herself slipping into the chaos but reminded herself: *get a grip. You're an officer in the Regulation. Hold it together, even if you feel like you can't.*

Selina found Zed with Warrah, pulling out Regulation weapons.

"What took you so long?" Warrah asked.

"Oh, trying to get the plan from the crew. I may as well have asked the airlock for its opinion."

Zed asked, "Did you see anything on bridge monitors on how bad it is?"

"At least five Omegan starcraft. Already took out one of our fighter escorts."

"What about Ellene?"

Selina struggled with the true answer to Zed's question. "She's gone. The *Dionysus* bailed."

"What?"

"They said the *Dionysus* took a lot of fire, maybe they took off to save themselves."

"Well, that's great. Guess there's nothing we can try that isn't riskier than what they're already doing," Zed replied.

"Of course, pulse rifles versus starcraft cannon isn't a fight at all, is it?" Selina asked.

"No, but the *Evangeline* has a few exploratory craft on board. They don't have firepower, but they're fast as hell." Warrah said.

"Can we even get to them?" Selina asked.

"Well, seeing as the UA's distracted, we've a good chance of that," Warrah said.

"We'd be zinging around out there trying not to get hit while everyone back here is helpless. Not an option." Zed shook his head.

Evangeline shook with a blast nearby. Shouts came over the onboard comm. "Taking fire, taking fire! Everyone shelter in place, brace for impact!"

Selina hunched, her back pressed against a crate. She hated being stuck like they were, but it was out of their control. They'd made a deal with the UA and had to wait it out until it was over.

The remaining Regulation officers showed up, filling out their group to twenty. While Warrah handed out weapons, Zed briefed the squad.

"First, activate your envirosuits. If they blast a hole in our side and we get sucked into space, you'll at least have 30 minutes to get to safety."

With a sly grin, Warrah thrust a pulse rifle toward Selina, which she gladly accepted.

Zed continued. "Second, I don't want us all bunched up. Since the UA is at least acting like they want to save the *Evangeline*, I want a small unit of me, Ravencraft, Nock, and Malek covering close to the main airlock. The rest, keep comms open and fall back further onto the ship. If you see UA troops, let them get into position, but don't let them push you too far out either. Beyond that, stay low. If you have contact, give 'em hell. The UA troops are the first line of defense. If you see one fall, fill the gap. Blast anyone in your way before they blast you. Remember, we are the Regulation. We adapt, overcome and survive!"

The group gave a resounding "HUUH!" in response.

As the other troops fell back into position, Selina, Zed, Warrah, and Ramsey made their way up the hallway. Soon, the thundering of footsteps rumbled behind them. A group of four UA troops passed, each of them with an activated pulse rifle in ready carry.

Selina flung her pulse rifle up as if to say *Hey morons, we've got weapons too.* Zed held the muzzle of her rifle down. "Don't bother. They're interested in saving the *Evangeline.* That's enough for now."

"You mean they're interested in not being sucked into space," Warrah countered.

"Whatever. The main airlock is straight ahead. Get behind cover somewhere close and wait. Any shooting starts, there'll be chances to join in."

To their front, near the airlock, the group of UA soldiers increased to ten and had formed a half circle around the entrance to *Evangeline.* Zed and Selina edged up nearby until they were twenty feet from the UA troops. They crouched behind storage crates that lined both sides of the corridor.

Selina bumped Warrah's fist, and they shared a grim smile. "Ready for this?"

"As I'll ever be," came Warrah's whispered response.

The *Evangeline's* main airlock let loose with a loud hiss and a series of loud grinding noises.

"This is it. Selina, take the right side. I'll cover left." Zed said.

Ramsey edged over to the side where Selina knelt while Warrah took the left side behind Zed. *Whoever comes through won't get by without a fight. They might want us, but they're gonna pay a lot for it.*

Assorted growling roared outside the airlock.

"Any of you ever see an Omegan up close?" Zed asked the group.

Warrah shrugged. "Mostly in training simulations."

Selina nodded. "A few, in skirmishes around Tas Ralong."

Ramsey said, "Nasty suckers. Look like walking lizards. They have a vital spot in the neck if you can zero on that between all that damn armor they usually wear."

Selina's stomach fluttered as they waited in the hallway. "You never end the fight, right Zed?"

Zed looked over with a proud smile as he gave Selina a quick thumbs up.

After another long moment, the airlock burst into a series of sparks, and the lights shut off again. Selina focused on the darkness and saw the glowing red eyes of their party. The UA troops let loose the first barrage. The blasts from weapon fire slammed into walls and created a spray of grayish Omegan blood before them. Selina activated her pulse rifle. The trademark whistle and momentary hum were a little comforting, a familiar sound in the middle of a desperate fight.

The air thickened with smoke. Selina heard Zed bellowing orders in the foggy cloud of dust and debris. Then, another UA troop let out a series of yells that ended in gurgling heaves.

Seeing Ramsey jump up, Selina edged forward, firing several short bursts.

"Zed!" Selina shouted, but no response. Finally, she stood enough that she saw a huge Omegan. This one was easily seven feet tall and covered in a series of armor and a helmeted enclosure. The Omegan let out a guttural growl as it trained eyes on Selina's. She froze in place.

Before she made any move of her own, she heard a series of shouts behind her, and there stood Farlane with several of the crew, firing on the Omegan intruders. Finally, the hulking Omegan gave up on Selina and surged past her on a one-way collision course with Farlane's group. The scene was a chaotic mix of weapons fire, swung and dismembered limbs, and assorted screams of agony. Finally, after several seconds of this, the towering Omegan stood alone in a pile of limbs that had once been Farlane and his crew.

Selina turned but found herself face to face with the barrel of an Omegan pistol. Her in-suit translator removed any doubt of what was happening.

"All Xeno drop weapons and place hands on head."

Chapter Twelve

THE OMEGANS MADE SHORT WORK of Ramsey and Warrah, leading them off onto their craft. However, Selina and Zed were brought face to face with Ve Bartosik. An imposing helmet topped off the Omegan commander's look. A dark steel set of battle armor with several char marks and etchings of an Omegan battle creed completed the ensemble. Ve's scaly, grimy face with deep red glowing eyes gave Selina more than she wanted as a focal point.

Selina watched Ve's large frame as he studied her in a visual dance with the first echelon who dared resist Omegan intrusion and capture.

"Welcome aboard Omegan starcraft *Praximus*. But, first, where's the captain of that ridiculous vessel we pulled you from?"

Selina eyed Zed for a moment. Then, finally, Zed said, "He's still aboard and unavailable. You should've talked with him before that big lug of yours ripped the whole crew into chopped meat."

Ve responded with a devious smile and snort. "They chose to resist. Besides, it shows again how well Omegans handle even the best the Universal Alliance can offer."

"You think a lot of yourself, don't you?" Selina muttered. Ve quickly moved in so close to her that Selina saw every pockmark in the nasty glare on the Omegan's face. His breath fogged her visor.

"Don't get smart, Xeno scum. You're lucky we got orders to take you alive, or you'd be limb stew like your UA friends right now." Ve looked Selina over like she was a load of rotten meat that needed disposal. "You know, some of our crew have been wondering just how fried Xeno tastes. Now then, before we stow you with the rest of our cargo, tell me... where is Ellene Ballo?"

"I don't know who you're talking about," Selina said.

Ve slammed his fist into Selina's chest. She yelped and stumbled backward onto the Omegan directly behind her. As quickly as she'd fallen, Selina was shoved back upright. A heavy soreness throbbed through Selina's core.

Ve leaned in closer to Selina. The rancid stench of Ve's breath permeated the filtration systems of her envirosuit and had her gag reflex in overdrive. "I'm not in the mood for games, Xeno. Tell me where she is before I hurt you where you don't get back up."

Zed said, "She went ahead of our convoy to scout."

Ve scowled for a moment. "We'll visit her soon enough," Ve growled a few moments longer before he swiped the air between him and Selina with a dismissive wave. "Put this filth with the rest in the hold below. I'm tired of their stench.

While they were grabbed and force marched down the hallway to the lower decks of *Praximus*, Selina's mind traveled between stabs of pain from the firm hold on her arms. Her hope of getting to planet Yassel and finally some long-term safety was gone. Ellene was pulled out of the picture along with the small team the UA sent as support.

Still, Selina clung to hope that Ket had seen her message. It was all she had, even if that was an interstellar pipe dream.

Chapter Thirteen

SELINA AND COMPANY SPENT THE REST of the voyage in a series of dank, dark, and smelly storage containers. Selina spent the first few hours wondering what formerly occupied their holding area that gave it such a foul effervescence.

Once the *Praximus* landed on Omegana, the captives were escorted through a series of rooms and industrial facilities. The air was musty and damp. Selina saw the Omegan crest in several places, including wall banners that stared back at Selina like an evil specter.

Their walk took them through a network of tunnels. Low lights gave slight visibility among the overall darkness. They passed alongside a mechanical area with loading docks that spewed toxic smoke into the air, dimly lit rooms with terminals and conveyors, and a chorus of metal screeching on metal. At least Selina hoped it was mechanical noise and not the screams of something in the darkness.

Soon they entered a large hall. A well-lit stage was the obvious focal point, and the stench Selina had experienced with Ve seemed to have been multiplied by a million. An ominous clamor filled the air, and she realized that there was a large crowd assembled, and clearly, she and her fellow captives were the featured item of the moment. Their escorts prodded them on their march toward the grandstand.

Several spotlights lit the darkened space just enough so a series of banners hung on either side of the main platform stood out as prominent. The two flags closest to the center had an identical crest on them, while the other two banners had some strange letters; Selina assumed some Omegan phrase on the order of "Tonight's Menu: Human."

On either side of the pathway they walked was a series of bleachers that rose forty feet above Selina and the others. The seating wrapped around and sloped upward to the ceiling, giving the design a Romanesque look. Omegan citizens filled the chairs, collectively bellowing a series of taunts, screeches, and other random snarls filled the stale air.

Selina spotted Warrah in the crowd, but too far away to talk. Selina's gut relaxed for a second until the shouts revved up again, and her belly tightened all the more.

When they arrived at the aisle's end, they were pushed up further until they were closer to the platform. The area wasn't large enough for them, but their group filled out the sides, and the rest were still back in the walkway behind Selina. A series of chimes sounded, and the assembled crowd began a chant. It was a series of clicks, hisses, insect-like noises, and whoops. The coordinated chant reverberated through the entire auditorium. Selina felt a chill go through her, wondering if the carol was a pre-slaughter signal. Her heartbeat throbbed in her neck. Zed looked to be holding his cool, but Selina noticed the beads of sweat on his forehead and face.

A booming voice echoed across the room from a series of nearby speakers. The masses responded to the booming voice with their refrain, in a sort of religious chorus.

A few sharp prods at the backs of Selina and the others, and they were walked over to the side of the stage. A group of Omegans stood at the center of the dais, wearing ceremonial cloaks.

Selina struggled against her wrist restraints, but she knew it was pointless. Ever since they'd arrived, she hadn't seen any less than double the amount of Omegans near her and her fellow captives. A cordon of troops stood before them, dressed differently than their initial escorts. The line of Omegans had more regal-looking armor, and their faces were shielded behind masks. Although Selina wondered what the point of the pomp was, she assumed their final destination included two stops: pain and suffering. Her eyes burned with sweat.

Finally, a loud tone sounded, followed by a disembodied voice. "Hail Emperor Zakmar."

All troops snapped to attention, which sent a roaring thunder of echoes through the hall. As punctuation to this, the Omegans yelped an Omegan phrase, some kind of salute, Selina assumed.

At the front of the hall, the line of Omegans split in two, each half separating to make an entrance for Emperor Zakmar. He strode in, a collection of capes swept behind him, an ornate helmet over his head, as the Omegans in the crowd continued their chorus of cheers and salutes. Selina hoped no one had noticed her eyes when they rolled.

Arriving on stage, Zakmar stood for a moment and savored the welcome before he thrust his hands up, silencing his obedient drones of an audience. "Today, we have received a gift, through the effectiveness of our Horde. You may wonder why I am so excited by the puny Xeno here. Our spies have informed us that Ellene Ballo wants to use the Xeno to build an army to attack Malone Stanton and Omegana. So, not only will we stop that from happening, but we will learn what about the Xeno makes them so valuable and use that against Ellene Ballo and the UA to destroy them both once and for all!"

Cheers abounded. Selina was struck in the back and doubled over, along with the rest of her party. Shortly after this came the bellowed cry, "Onto the stage, Xeno!"

Selina caught the Omegans behind them, blunt staves in their hands and glances that were neither welcoming nor patient. She looked at Zed, whose eyes were as narrow as she'd ever seen them. "Gonna teach these asses some manners when I get a chance."

"Shh," Selina replied.

Soon, their group was front and center, with nothing between them and Zakmar. The compliment of Omegan troops flanking their leader presented their weapons as a not-so-subtle reminder that any escape attempts were likely to be suicide.

Zakmar was dressed in regal robes. His skin was above average in scaliness by Omegan standards, and his reddish glowing eyes added a cold fury to his face. His mouth was turned into a terrifying grin.

"I understand Ellene Ballo isn't with your group." Zakmar scowled. "It's time she and the Nara learn along with the UA that Omegans control Ling Galaxy. Any movement around Ling Galaxy, including one for your people, is prohibited unless I approve it. So, welcome to Omegana. I want you all to enjoy the rest of your short lives. You can make the rest of your time easier on yourselves by doing exactly what you're told."

Selina tensed as their group was led off. She struggled against the forced march, but it was useless and only got her another rap, this time on the cheek.

A sharp jab hit Selina in the side, and she looked in the snarling face of an Omegan holding a spear toward her. "Move it, Xeno. You're headin' for our prison. You might wanna think of it as your gravesite."

Chapter Fourteen

S ELINA AND THE NEWEARTH CAPTIVES were brought to an Omegan holding facility. The buildings were as dark and cold as they'd seen since their arrival on Omegana. Smells of decaying flesh hung in the air.

They were placed in a series of cells, each of them sized for groups of 40. Once locked in, a series of periodic feedings went on for several days. The meals, such as they were, involved little more than several containers of barely identifiable items that resembled some sort of meat and liquid with a strong metallic taste. Eventually, their excess hunger dulled the average palettes enough that accepting the dubious protein intake wasn't so crazy anymore.

Selina wasn't sure how long this routine went. With no windows to even guess the time, the length of their stay was measured mainly by periodic visits with food.

Throughout the time, Selina kept regular contact with Zed. With the only clear access point to their location the single door used by the guards, it was pretty clear their escape wouldn't happen without a lot of luck and outside help.

The increasing amount of facial hair on her fellow male inmates,

Zed especially, was one more thing that gave Selina a loose idea of time passage.

Zed pawed at his beard. "This has to be the longest I've ever grown this."

Selina smirked. "Just when I thought you were ugly enough."

Zed responded with an amused glare. "So, what do you make of Zakmar's line about making us an army?"

"Well, it's not that different than what Ellene was telling me she wanted for us. I think no matter what happens, we're worth something to both sides. As long as they don't blow us up in the crossfire, anyway."

They shared a brief chuckle at their fix, but their quick moment stopped when the lights dimmed. A collection of dull thumps shook the ground, and klaxons blared outside.

"Any chance that's about us?"

"Maybe," Zed replied. "Maybe Ellene sent a distress call."

"You don't think she got wasted?"

"Naah. Not by them, anyway. There's a reason behind it, but I can't figure that out. As for whatever's happening out there, I say anything bad for the Omegans is good for us."

Selina thought how nice it would've been if they were armed. They just had to hope that whatever happened, they could get over on a guard soon and get out of their collective mess.

The noises outside were a cacophony of engines from starcraft, blasts from cannon and small weapons fire, and an assortment of shouting. It was anyone's guess, though, how it was going and just what it all meant for their situation.

An idea jumped into Selina's mind, and she grabbed Zed for a quick chat about it, but a loud clang quickly stopped her plan at the end of the hallway. Of all the unrecognizable sounds, she could've picked out that one anywhere. It was the main hatch entrance to their holding area. Soon afterward, a line of emergency lights cast a subtle glow in the hallway, enough that Selina made out the faint outlines of

Omegans who walked down, and then she heard the voice of a female Omegan.

"Attention, Xeno prisoners. My name is Charista Mantisword. In a moment, your cell doors will open. You'll then file into the corridor and form a single file line. Guards will direct you from there. Do not, I repeat, do not do anything other than follow their exact instructions, or you will be shot on sight and left to die here."

Selina managed a low sigh as she followed suit with the rest of the prisoners and was escorted out of the holding area. Their trip took a series of turns and even involved a walk along a narrow catwalk amid heavy piping stretched in either direction for miles.

Soon, they arrived at an underground rail transport and were escorted into some heavy-duty windowless cargo containers. There weren't any seats, so the order of the moment was to fit in so the Omegans could close the doors. Unfortunately, Selina had gotten mixed up in the shuffle and was separated from Zed.

Despite being in close proximity to the others, Selina felt as alone as she'd ever been, and for the first time in a while, real fear crept over her and sat with her like a most unwelcome guest.

They rode for several hours. Charista met them once their ride ended, and escorted them to another facility, and they were again brought to holding areas, though these were much nicer than before.

Charista said, "You are now resident products of the Omegan Science Wing. You'll be brought out one at a time or in groups, what-ever the need calls for. Until then, relax, and know your true purpose is about to be discovered."

Selina edged closer to Zed. There were so many questions and no answers, but Selina needed at least to vent her confusion.

"Zed, were we pawns all along? Maybe Ellene and the UA needed us for something, and they don't anymore?"

Zed took a deep breath and looked ahead as their group was marched deeper into a well-lit building filled with monitor screens along the walls.

What seemed so simple just weeks earlier had become another

labyrinth of the unknown. Being a prisoner of Omegana was nothing Selina imagined when listening to Ellene's grand ideas about Essence and what it meant for her future and those of NewEarth. Whatever came from their situation, they were a piece in a larger game, and her fear for their survival chances had never been greater.

Suddenly, Selina felt Zed's arm around her shoulders. The light was dim, but not so much that she couldn't see Zed's tired but determined glance.

"You never end the fight, Selina."

The Essence Wars Series
All of these titles are available individually on Amazon.com

Xeno Reckoning (novelette)
Gambit of Dares (novelette)
Quest for Dominion (novelette)
Quantum of Destiny (novelette)
Vengeance Directive (novelette)
Balance of Retribution (novelette)
Revenge Nexus (novelette)
Stratagem Awakening (novelette)
Collateral Crisis (novelette)

Have you read the Valkyrie Chronicles Series?

Forced into a life she hates by the government of Lebabolis, the last human nation on Earth, Ana Crucinal must comply with her pre-ordained future or undergo Realignment. But when her brother falls ill, Ana joins up with the resistance in an attempt to flee Lebabolis—only to learn that the true threat lies elsewhere: an alien race known as the Omegans. All of this was foreseen. A thousand years ago a man living in New Orleans had imagined the future Ana now lives in. He wrote about the resistance, the alien menace, everything. Desperate to save themselves and the remnants of the human race, the resistance formulates a plan to do the only thing they can think of: travel back in time to save the future.

With her enemies closing in, Ana knows this is her one chance to save herself, her brother, and the resistance. Failure is death and the never-ending enslavement of humanity.

Buy the books of the Valkyrie Chronicles Series on Amazon today and find out why so many have fallen in love with Ana and her mission.

Have you read the Valkyrie Chronicles Series?

Menace Ascending (short story prequel)
Cataclysm Epoch (novel)
Settling Darkness (novel)
Valkyrie Rising (novel)
The Valkyrie Chronicles Complete Series (novel, box set)

The Essence Wars Continue!

Crucible of Legacy, the first FULL LENGTH novel in the Essence Wars Series, is coming soon! Get ready to hear the story of Pierce Sava, son of the current ruler of the Universal Alliance, Nic Sava. Pierce had more than a few disagreements on how things were run, and decided it best he went his own way, in the wilds of Ling Galaxy. Employed by the Syndicates, Pierce is content with his life of running cargoes and mixing it up with his friend Ket Durban. But, when the UA and Nic Sava face a crisis, can Pierce find it within himself to return to the life and the love he left behind, to help the UA restore their crumbling order as the Essence Wars rage on?

About the Author

Paul Heingarten spreads time between writing, being a musician, and, since 2002, a career in Information Technology. He lives in the southern United States with his wife Andrea.

Other Titles by Paul Heingarten

The Harvest (short story)

Leave from Absence (novel)

The Monitor (short story)

Natural Election (short story)

Cataclysm Epoch (novel)

Settling Darkness (novel)

Valkyrie Rising (novel)

Menace Ascending (short story)

Xeno Reckoning (novelette)

Gambit of Dares (novelette)

Quest for Dominion (novelette)

Quantum of Destiny (novelette)

Vengeance Directive (novelette)

Balance of Retribution (novelette)

Destination Exodus (short story)

Revenge Nexus (novelette)

Stratagem Awakening (novelette)

Collateral Crisis (novelette)

www.ingramcontent.com/pod-product-compliance
Lightning Source LLC
Chambersburg PA
CBHW071250250626
47163CB00002B/408